# Mr. Mehan's
## Mildly Amusing Mythical
# Mammals

# Mr. Mehan's
## Mildly Amusing Mythical
# Mammals

### A Hypothetical Alphabetical

By Matthew Mehan

Illustrated by John Folley

TAN Books
Charlotte, North Carolina

Library of Congress Cataloging-in-Publication Data

Names: Mehan, Matthew, author. | Folley, John, illustrator.
Title: Mr. Mehan's mildly amusing mythical mammals : a hypothetical
    alphabetical / Matthew Mehan ; illustrated by John Folley.
Description: Charlotte, North Carolina : TAN Books, [2018]
Identifiers: LCCN 2018027401 | ISBN 9781505112498 (hardcover)
Subjects:  LCSH: Animals, Mythical--Poetry.
Classification: LCC PS3613.E4 M7 2018 | DDC 811/.6--dc23
LC record available at https://lccn.loc.gov/2018027401


Published in the United States by
TAN Books
PO Box 410487
Charlotte, NC 28241
www.TANBooks.com

*In loving thanks for our fathers, our mothers, our wives, our children, and our friendship.*

—Matthew Mehan & John Folley

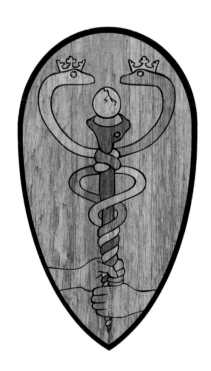

# O What Creatures!

Ah come refrain
your sight
the eye and 5 senses
behold
instead
mammals
roving
unfenced
some herded
some long fanged
and howling
some wheeling out
into the bright
green blue world

# The Dark

"Afraid of the dark? Not I!" I cried.
And cried and cried and cried did I.
For while I cried, the monsters spied
That why I cried was because I swore
I felt some monster fuzz,
In the dark, lightly applied it was,
To the night-shirt that I wore.
So as I laid me in my bed,
"Of the dark, I'm not afraid," I said—or rather cried;
And cried and cried and cried did I.

# A Note to All Children Readers

Good, good! Warm welcome to you all! I want to tell you that there is—it's true!—a very best way to read these mildly amusing mythical mammals. Read them *to* someone you love. Many of these mammals are funny, and some are scary. And the first of them has a name that's fairly impossible to say. But it's best to try anyway. You and whomever you are reading to can crack each other up and flub the funky words, or turn the page and say, "That one's for the birds!" And in the back of the book, you can find a few games and a glossary, for names and words you might not know. I even put the word "glossary" in the glossary, just for show. Read well! And listen carefully.

# A Note to All Adult Readers
### (The Fine Print)

We all love lions, but we all hate pride. "Adult" readers may well be denied. I suggest you try your best to become a child once more. Doing so will bring you through poetry's locked door. Now. When you're ready, hold the book steady, raise your eyes from here, then reread the note that's truly true, the one to All Children Readers, which you thought, perhaps, was not addressed to you?

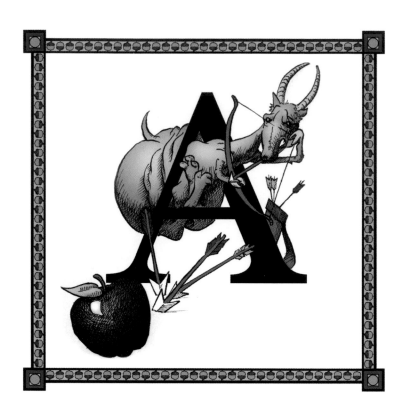

## What's an Ango?

The Ango has but little fame,
Because folks hate its proper name:
"ANG–o–GROB–u–GUNK–a–LUNG–stis"
Has a ring that most find unctuous.
And worse, the Ango has a look
That fits the awful name it took.
The Angogrobugunkalungstis
Is only loved by utter dunces,
Who like to use long Latin words,
When pointing out the plainest birds:
"Corvus–brachyrhynchos"
and "Cardinalis–cardinalis"
Are what Ango-lovers like to call
The common crow and cardinal.
So when your Latin troubles you,
And you forget just where your tongue is,
Thank God for words of common use,
Like "Ango" for "Angogrobugunkalungstis."

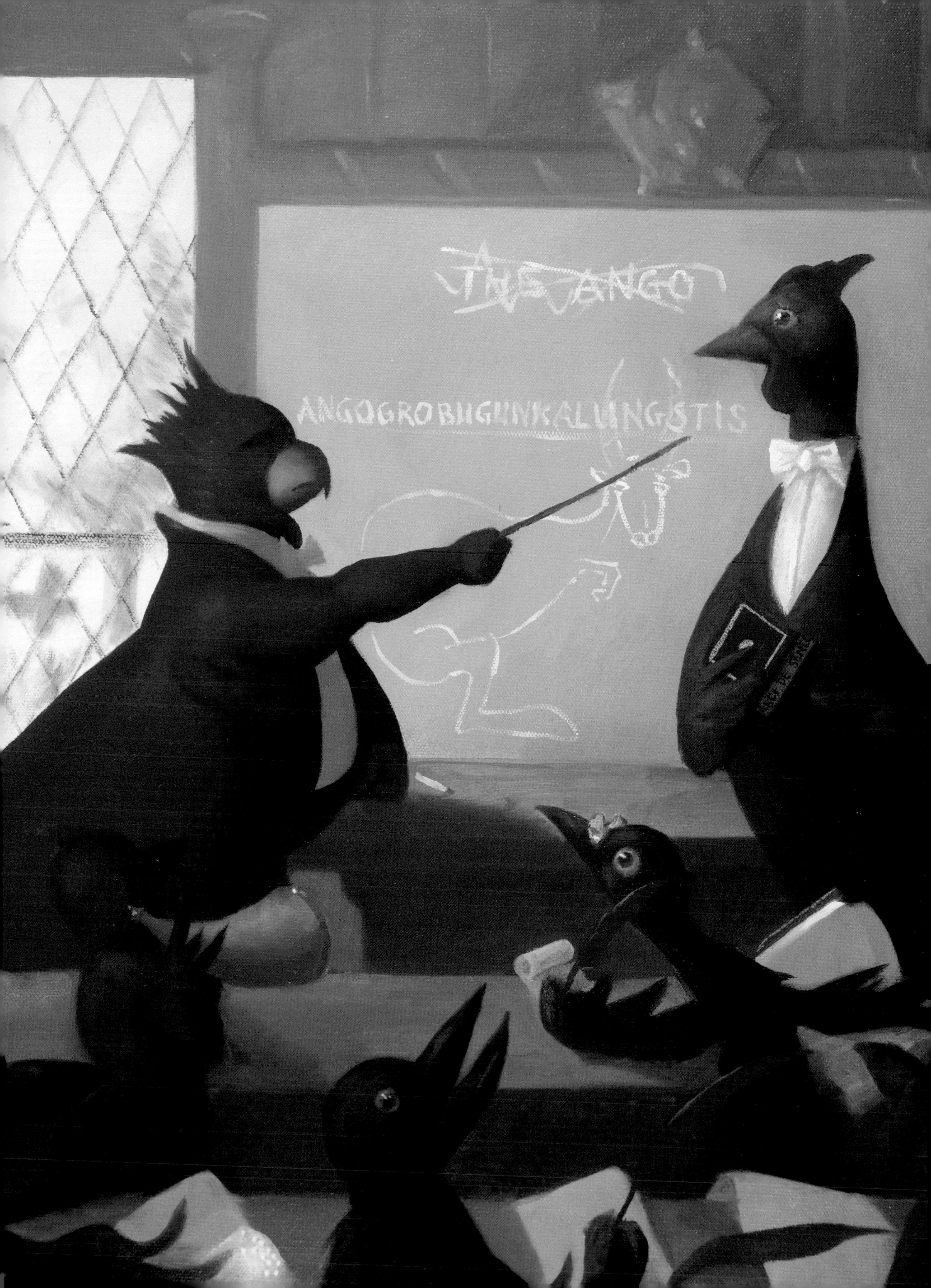
ANGOGROBUGUNKALUNGSTIS

## The Blug

Bumbling by as slow as a slug,
Is the tubbiest creature known as the Blug.
The Blug plods a humorous pace,
So slow, in fact, that he came in third place,
Against the tortoise and the hare,
Who at the finish line stood and stared
At this blobular, jolly, gelatinous jug,
As across the sky his body he lugged,
On the tiniest wings that the world's yet seen:
They're both the size of a kidney bean!
Why the Blug's quite a slug, but he seems not to care,
As he happily chugs through the cumbersome air.

## The Colvaino

The Colvaino eats rocks deep down in the earth,
He's a creature of some considerable girth:
Thick, fat legs and claws like the mole's,
For digging his den and his surfacing hole.
The entrance is wide like an elephant's rear,
And smells just as foul if you dare to draw near.
The Colvaino's quite picky, turning some rocks away,
"This one's too icky, that one's too gray"—
And oh, by the way, the Colvaino belches fire,
So meeting one's not something one should desire.
Yes, beware the Colvaino, as his rocks he slurps,
And run for your lives if ever he burps.

## The Dally

Among the pelting drops of rain,

The Dally can be seen again.

The rocks, the trees, they know him well,

But where he'll show no one can tell.

For though the forest's soaked and sopped,

The Dally skirts each drop that's plopped.

So if you are one keen of eye,

Who sits and stoops in storms, you'll spy

The dodgy Dally dancing dry.

## The Evol

*(...speaks to the Dally)*

Behold a troglodytic ape,

With grimy locks and eyes agape.

Or rather not agape per se,

For his eyes have long since fallen away.

The Evol is his caving name.

In caves his eyes grew slowly lame:

First colors failed, then by degrees,

The shadows showed whate'er he pleased.

The sockets of his eyes remain.

He claims they cause him zero pain.

An ape within an inky space,

Whose eyes concaves long since replaced.

"Either I or it is raining. I fear
dampness in that cave will be the death of me.
I feel spongy, drippy—my body weeps—
the cold has dripped from stalactites. They hang like teeth
hidden in a dark mouth, one that drools as
old fools do in homes long forgotten.

"I have lost myself, excuse me, Dally.
What I meant to say is either I or
it—'it' as in the sky—is weeping from on high.
I do not think, of course, that the sky could be weeping—
no, no. I can see the sky in spite
of lacking both my eyes, with a science most wise.

"Disbelieve me, Dally? Close your eyes and
see what I myself will whisper in the rain:
the things you cannot see cause so much pain.
Feel the soil beneath your paws: roots and
worms you know, but fungi also grow and
creep invisible filaments of death, and so
without breath they say, 'I LOVE NOT YOU.'"

> The Evol ape now felt warm rain,
> That tapped tenderly his leathery brain.
> The Dally slowed, and stopped, and sat,
> And with the Evol had a chat.

"Or I could take these wet, black boughs—
take one, take it, touch and feel it now, if you
like. Either it did or didn't yet or it
never will flower, but it matters not.
Only an hour will it last in the vastness
of time. Even if it flowered, the secrets of its power
aren't ours. It mocks us: 'I LOVE NOT YOU.'"

"Nay, think beyond this tree's swollen
husk, if you still brusquely deny my theme, for
above this black raincloud and beyond the
unsubstantial light of day, oceans of
darkness lie. None can breathe in that waste of
space. Why such a place? If not to make the
fearful case: 'I LOVE NOT YOU.'

"Miserly stars break up the mantle of the expanding
night; they cast off fire, which cooled to thoughtless
dust, which pooled as a ball of rust, which foolishly
has ended thus, with unintended us—
O speak not! The world weeps, besot with
pain, which I wrongly call rain. The dark stars
their orphans mar with an 'I LOVE NOT YOU.'"

> The Evol had been weeping, from his sockets deep,
> tears that through his fur had seeped,
> down his chin, down his chest—
> drip, drip, on the Dally they came to rest.
>
> Twice wetted, by the tears and the rain,
> which long before the tears refrained,
> the Dally opened up his eyes
> and silently began to rise.
>
> The Dally sadly slunk away,
> Feeling something less than gay.
> The Evol did not stop his words,
> but blindly spoke to the indignant birds.
>
> O Dally, do not dally long,
> nor by heart rehearse that Evol's song!
> On tears like his, still take no chance,
> though you may weep, provided you dance!

## The Fáh-la-las

*(...sing to the dolorous Dally)*

In winter the children are often misled,

As visions of Christmas lights dance overhead.

Mothers are human, and fathers forget

to say to their littles what ought to be said.

And that makes for children who simply don't know

that when pine boughs grow heavy with holiday snow,

In the trees there are creatures whose joy is to glow,

Blinking distinctly a winter rainbow.

Children will point at their colors with awe,

And think that electrical light's what they saw.

Alas, with their silence mamás and papás

Will fail to speak of the wee Fáh-la-las.

But look—I mean listen!—now is your chance!

On the glistening snow, the bright Fáh-la-las dance.

Sing in their songs they still sing as they prance:

The Fáh-la-la la-láh, la-láh-láh chants.

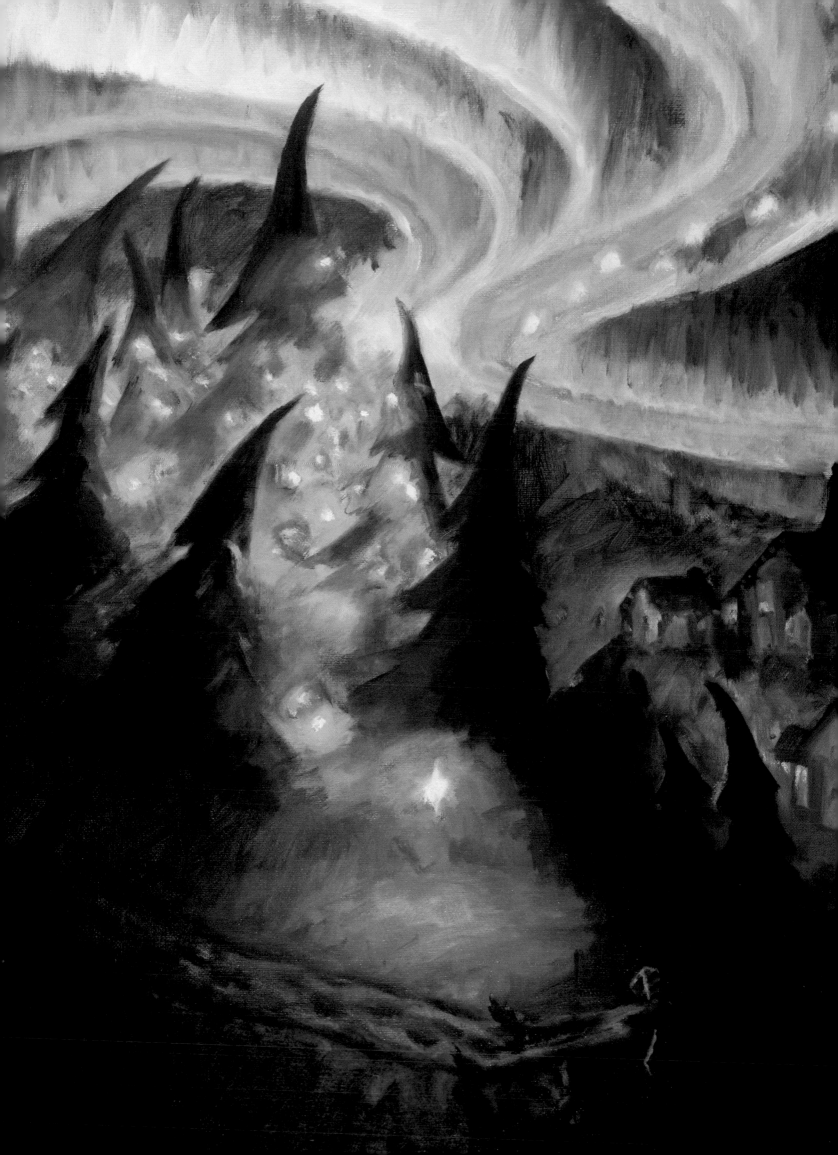

## The Gallant and the Golden Birch

This creature is aged, gray, and good,
and I've seen him walking in the deep wood.
Twenty summers ago, where the old birch stood,
the Gallant overtook me as only he could,
with a "pardon me," and an "if I may,"
minding the mint leaves and picking his way.
He stopped at the old birch and gently his hand
patted that tree's curlicue bands.

"Mr. Birch," the Gallant asked, "how do you do?
I've come from Turtle Bay just to see you.
Blueberry Hill's looking very blue,
Though the bear cubs have eaten more than a few."
The golden birch—an *old* birch, mind you now—
made a sweeping, gallant, golden bow
that bent his grand canopy down,
and touched green to gray, crown to crown.

"Mr. Birch," the Gallant smiled,
"it's so good to meet you out here in the wild.
I recall a sapling and a Gallant child
met on this day and played for a while."
And as the Gallant spoke these words,
his friend received a flock of birds.
"I see you've got company to wait on;
I'd best not stand here and prate on."

Old Mr. Birch seemed somehow to nod.
For the Gallant and him, this was nothing odd.

# A Few Hai-chus

*(...teach the Dally a thing or two)*

### 1

Ah, morn's mist and cool,
shade and blossom. Bright light shafts
hit the Hai-chus' eyes.

### 2

Ah, pause. Ah, crinkled
snouts. Ah, blasting sneeze shakes loose
Hai-chus' wet and fleece.

### 3

Choose what happens to
you. Greet sun-kissed sneezes with a
Hai-chu's "yes, I do."

# The Inowallah

*(...call to the Dally)*

Walking through deep jungle paths,
Passing cool and trickling baths,
Footfalls pressing loamy earth,
In our mythic place of birth—
This and more is done in search,
Of the Inowallah's perch.
Up in tree-tops old as seas,
Swaying in a tropic breeze,
Giving out its haunting call,
To the other Inowall.
Inowallahs form a pair,
Rock together in the air,
Cock their heads and prick an ear
Whenever a searcher ventures near.
Inowallah tails are long,
Like a periegetic song.
That means seekers on the ground
See two tails come floating down:
One is royal bluish-brown,
The other's red and soft as down.

Inowallahs know the pain
Seekers take to come through rain,
Nettle, heat, and hardships great,
Just to find a treed primate.
Cries of pity fill the air,
As if to say, "you're finally there!"
Hoping seekers leave with glee,
Inowallahs let them see—
Not themselves—they don't descend
—Nonetheless, they deign to send
Flowing tails of blue and red,
Down to touch the heart and head.
Many fail and in despair,
Sit and pout and clutch their hair.
Many will not touch a tail,
Though the Inowallahs' wail
Beckons them to search once more,
Struggling through the forest floor:
"Inowallah, wallah way."
"Don't give up," they seem to say.

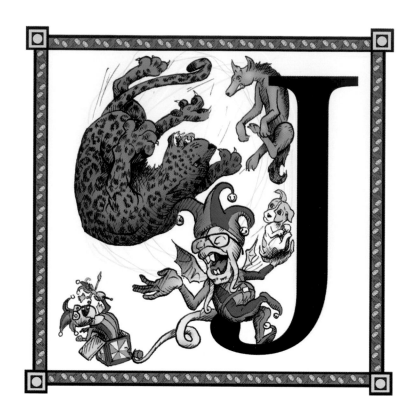

# The Jargontalky

*(...confuses the Blug)*

'Twas thrilling, and to slippery rows
His wily, nimble panel gave:
All whimsy were the droves & droves
Of new rules how to behave.

"Beware the Jargontalk, my son!
Old laws it spites, old laws rehashed.
Beware the Hubbub words, and run
To luminous Candor's stash!

"We took these corpulent words in hand:
Long time we ransomed truth besot—
But bested we the Jargontalk:
We spoke less than we thought.

"But, as in oafish thought we sat,
The Jargontalk, with lies of fame,
Came whispering as if understood
—Obscurity regained!

"O you! O you! You're through and through
Morbid, laden, yet truth you lack!
You've left some dead, or full in the head
Of humbug they spew back.

"And how will we slay the Jargontalk?
What be the arms, the verbal toys?!
Don't fragment love from what you say,
nor truth, nor light, nor joys!"

'Twas thrilling, and to slippery rows
His wily, nimble panel gave:
All whimsy were the droves & droves
Of new rules how to behave.

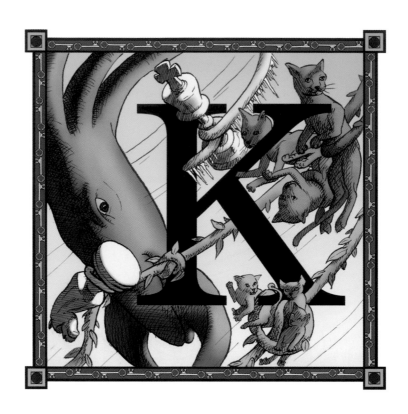

# Kalondahres

*(...dizzies the Dally)*

Kalondahres, Kalondahres,
Always round and round you go always.
Kalondahres, Kalondahres,
Always round and round you go.

Topsy-turvy in a flurry
Kalondahres spins around,
Never knowing where he's going,
Whether up the hill or down.

"Whether up the hill or down it,
Kalondahres, can you see?"
"No I'm sorry, very sorry,"
Kalondahres said to me.

"I see whirling, I see twirling,
I see blurring browns and greens.
But my journey's elevation?
That's a thing I've never seen."

Kalondahres, Kalondahres,
Always round and round you go always.
Kalondahres, Kalondahres,
Always round and round you go.

Then I asked the Kalondahres
Why he gasped and gulped for air:
"With each turn you seem to totter;
Are you tired or worn with care?"

"I've spun far," said Kalondahres,
"And there's farther still to go,
And with every revolution
The more tired do I grow."

"Like a climber climbing up through
Thinning air and deepening snow?"
But he only twirled away with
"I am sorry I don't know."

Topsy-turvy in a flurry
Kalondahres spins around,
Never knowing where he's going,
Whether up the hill or down.

Kalondahres, Kalondahres,
Always round and round you go always.
Kalondahres, Kalondahres,
Always round and round you go.

## The Lundregun

*(...sees the Dally and the Blug)*

Little is known of the Lundregun beast,
For no one's survived, who's seen 'em at least.
Deep in the watery depths he stews,
Befouling the water and meat that he chews.
And the sailor beset by the chills and the fits,
Knows well that the Lundregun under him sits,
For his stomach grows sick with the undulate sea,
That the creature increases in hopes two or three
Of the seamen go sailing right over the rails,
Where the hungering Lundregun's hundreds of tails
Will scoop up a few shipmen scared for their lives,
Then the Lundregan once again under them dives.

## A Mixxy Among the Reeds

A midnight Mixxy waded out
   And wriggled his pale white toes:
"This inky pool makes star-fire cool
   To the touch of my pale white toes."

With dainty digits, he dabbed the dark
   And blinking shimmers of fire,
And watched the ripples shake the skies,
   Lapping his toes in the mire.

"Kings have killed for lesser thrones
   Than this my fiefdom grand;
For who but I can claim to own
   The stars on which I stand?"

"Tu-wit, Tu-who!" from above the pool
   An unseen owl agreed—
The Mixxy darted out of sight,
   And sung among the reeds.

## The Nólle

*(...sees the Dally in his basket)*

My powers aren't store enough to relay
The tale of the Nólle.
    No lore of mine displays,
No late acquired folly,
    No liméd nightingale's
Dolorous song recalls,
    The reasons for such sorrow,
    Which flows as from a spring,
    Unearthed by wingless myth,
    Wherein sad shepherds sing.

The Nólle, almost as old as days,
In tears she bathes.
    She will not rise to meet you,
From her pool of lachrymose.
    She will not smile or greet you,

Nor quit her wistful repose.
  She will not cease her tolling
  Sobs that rise and burst,
  Like bubbles from the fen,
  In which she is immersed.

This is all she'll ever endeavor to say:
"O Nólle, Nólle!
  Why did you not turn away,
From the grievesome and unnatural?
  From the sweetness happenstantual?
From the tears that fell eventually,
  Surrounding me in an eddy
  of weeping, in a weir of weakness,
  —O my poor heart beneath
  a lymph of tears hard pressed!"

And with this fitful sorrowing lay,
Up heaves the Nólle,
  Above the salty loch,
Above its woeful rim,
  Above the weight of weeping,
A single, slender limb,
  Which weakly reaches up,
  Like one who's doomed to drown,
  Then willy-nilly grasps about,
  Then slowly lowers down.

## The Oominoos

*(...sings above the Dally and the Blug)*

Have you never entered a room
   and assumed you're alone?
But soon, a feeling moves in you,
   and in the room too,
So the hair on your head bristles like a broom?
     (because of whom?)
Have you ever discovered a tomb
   in a hazy coomb,
Where ages weigh heavy in the shady blooms?
   Cicadas thrum,
And you presume a soul has come,
     to loom, and to hum.
You might climb through the misty gloom,
   to a mountain subsumed
In plumes of cloud, which groomed in shroud
   a hallowed place
That makes all the world seem a lonely tomb?
     (or a stale room?)
Your five senses, if they fight the soul,
    conceal the numinous.
And your heart, if pure and light and whole,
    reveals the Oominoos.

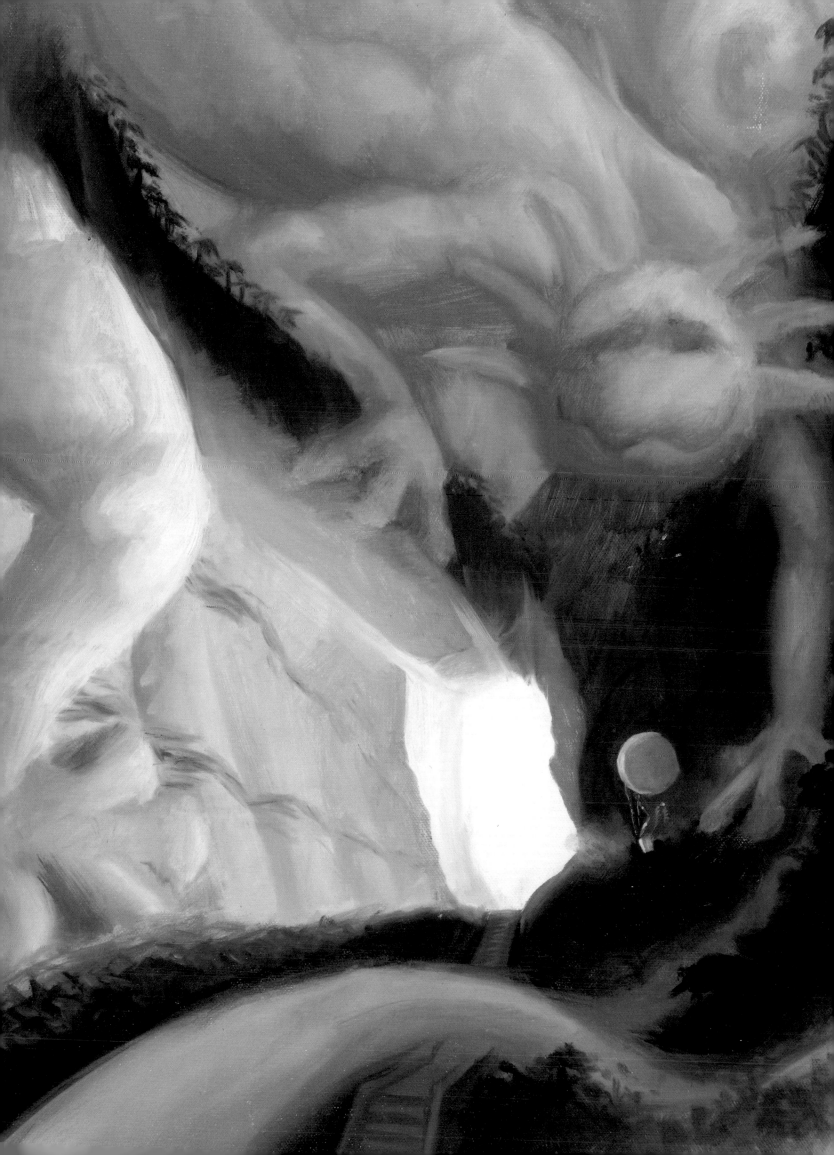

## The Plee

*(...pesters the Dally)*

Consider the sound of a billion bees,
Then add the crash of a thousand seas,
Next imagine the blue jay's scream,
But times'd by twelve, or so it would seem;
Add to that a piglet's squeal,
Only louder, like a siren's peal,
And then you've just begun to see
How loud the tiny Plee can be.
But see the Plee you never will,
When with his wail your ears he'll fill,
With a deafening, wild and wonton
"WHEEEEEEEEEEEEEEEEEEE!"
Till you stop, and you plead,
"WHAT DO YOU WANT FROM ME?!"
And then the flea-like screeching Plee,
Will stop his scream and set you free.

## The Wooly-Quilled Quecámbia

The Wooly-Quilled Quecámbias are queerly distinct:
they're mythical mammals, and now quite extinct.
Most other mammals thought Quecámbias brave
for quitting existence to avoid getting shaved.
The Quecámbias, you see, had everything arranged—
Everything, that is, until everything changed.

"You cannot shave the Wooly-Quilled Quecámbias!
We roam the chilled plains and fill the savánnias.
True, there used to be ice well north of Patagónia,
And—come to think of it—south of South Dakótia.
True, the snow used to fall for six months in Indiánia,
And that also holds true for dear ole Louisiánia.
Now I even overheat when I winter in Montania,
And yes, grandma expired on our trek to Texarkania—
But shaving my mane? It's completely insania!
I'm the glorious, strong-willed Wooly-Quilled Quecámbia!"

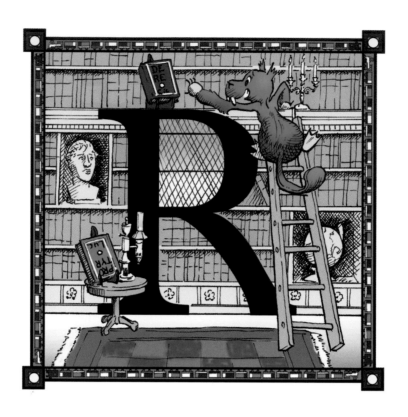

## The Rare

*(...eludes the Jargontalky)*

The hope of many hunters
Is to catch and kill the Rare.
Its meat is very tender;
They can sell its silky hair.
Its teeth are sold for jewelry,
Its tusks make microchips,
And hunters swear it truly,
"Locals eat its pickled lips!"
Its blood, it's thought by many,
Is a substitute for oil,
And its tongue will make you money
If you bury it in the soil.
But to catch and kill this mammal
Takes great care and greater toil,
For the dusty desert camel
Would soon begin to broil,
In the deadly desert places

Where the Rare's as cool as shade,
In the deadly desert places
Where the fates of fools are made.

Yet who can blame a hunter
Set to catch and kill the Rare?
True, to find one is a wonder,
And yes, no one's caught a pair.
Come to think, why it's been ages
Since they've spotted one at all...
So then the rarest Rares in cages,
Kept alive and kept in stalls,
Are worth more than Rares the hunters
Try to sell and gut and kill.
Well, then send along with hunters
Men with zoologic skill.
They can catch and keep the creature
And make tiny desert spaces
Where the Rare can be observed.
Yes, build tiny desert places
Where the sciences are served!
Where the rarest Rares in nature
Can be carefully preserved.
Once they find a Rare in nature
And put it in a stall,
We can charge the public money
And some days not charge at all!
We can film it being funny
And then sell the videos.
We could charge a giant fare
And say, "Hey, that's how it goes."
But only if the Rare stays rare
And everybody knows:

That the hope of many hunters
Is to catch and kill the Rare.
That its meat is very tender;
It has costly, silky hair.
That its teeth are sold for jewelry,
And its tusks make microchips,
And that hunters swear it truly,
"Locals eat its pickled lips!"
That its blood, it's thought by many,
Is a substitute for oil,
And that its tongue will make you money
If you bury it in the soil.

## To Be Like the Sillymede

*(...as dreamed by the Dally)*

As when a herd of jiggly hamsters
Goes giggling across a field,
Or like a flabby gam of whales
Swimming in Jello congealed:
Imagine a cat rolling in fat,
The Sillymede's something or other like that.

How like a buffalo heavy with lard,
Or like an old hound dog out in the yard;
As when a plump man is unable to rise
Out of his chair on account of his size:
Picture a rat that's too fat for a trap,
The Sillymede's somewhere near that on the map.

The Sillymede flails and flops as it goes,
Like a floundering fish that's got air up its nose,
As a jellyfish pools in the cup of the hand,

Just so will the Sillymede squish and expand:
Imagine a bat that's too fat for the air,
And now with the Sillymede quickly compare.

So silly of me to liken for you!
The Sillymede's far beyond simile's view,
For so far you readers still haven't a clue,
Whether this silly beast has got one eye or two:
Except that whatever that Sillymede's not,
What a silly degree of fat he has got.

## The Tale of the Tanglis

The Tanglis bull seems water-bound.
He has no legs for walking 'round,
Nor fins to flap as sea beasts do
Who come ashore a time or two
To meet a mate and rear their pups
And fetch a fish when family sups.

The Tanglis female dwells in snow.
She shuns the shores and lakes below.
On mountaintop she hopes for young,
In air too thin for human lungs.
For the pups she carves a warmish place
But limbless, does so with her face!

Who can recount her Tanglis pain?
To dig this way through ice and rock?!
To see her suffer—O the shock!
No more, no more! I must refrain.
Yet note that when she's made a dent,
The Tanglis bull starts his ascent.

The bulbous, blubberous Tanglis bull,
Who in the waves was meant to roll,
Must haul his bulk beyond the shore
To undertake his greatest chore:
With neither leg nor arm nor tail,
Up jagged mount the bull must flail.

O' Tanglis, Tanglis, Tanglis work!
Scrunch your blubber, shake and jerk!
Heave and sweat, gasp and strain,
Climb for months in freezing rain.
Could you, dear reader, long sustain
This woeful song of Tanglis pain?

The cow, she digs; the bull he scales.
Her rocky face begins to wail.
The wind it whips, the snow it falls.
The cow, the bull, each other calls.
The two have met on icy peak,
And there recover for a week.

At length two pups, one boy, one girl,
Are introduced into the world.
They drink the milk the cow secretes,
While with her bulk the den she heats.
The pups the bull invigorates
With rock fish he regurgitates.

And when the sun makes longer days,
The pups and parents all part ways:
The bull and boy-pup quiver down
To each their separate feeding ground;
The she-pup leaves her mother's breast,
And seeks a peak that suits her best.

The Tanglis pups will grow for years,
Forgetting Tanglis parents' tears,
And yet when Tanglis pups are grown,
This Tanglis task will be their own.
And reader, if this beast seems silly,
Thank me not. 'Twas nothing, really.

## The Noble Myth of the Urnaz, King of the Beasts

"You are an astonishing beast!"
Cry the fearful people facing east.
"You are an astral lord!"
Sings the sycophantic horde.
"You are an asp, an eagle,
An ascendant king, a sovereign regal!"

And bending down, the masses say,
"In awe we all must turn away;
For who can face so bright a day?
Therefore, we bow away from you;
But thus, we give you what you're due!"
And so the Urnaz preens and gloats,
As praises rise from thronging throats:

"O unassayable assizer!
Your assotting asterism!
O aseptic, assumental

66

master of asteism!
O arsis, O astheny!
O Urnaz, you are an astrogeny!"

And as the Urnaz listens well,
His beastly pride begins to swell.
Feeling this, he bids them cease.
But then he fears "the civil peace
May break if they stopped spelling out
Urnastic praises they must now shout!"

Las Vaquitas Lullaby

Con Anima ♩=105

Matthew Mehan

La lu lay, la lu la, Las Va-qui--tas,

la lu lay, la lu la, Las Va-qui--tas.

O so few, O so beau-ti-ful la--dies, Tell me true, Las Va-qui-tas,

whe-re are your ba--bies. La lu lay, la lu la, Las Va-qui--tas,

la lu lay, la lu la, Las Va-qui--tas. O-ceans blue

are for you and your ba--bies O I'll be true to you --, you beau-ti-ful

la--dies. La lu lay, la lu la, Las Va-qui--tas,

la lu lay la lu la, Las Va-qui--tas.

# The Double Vólle

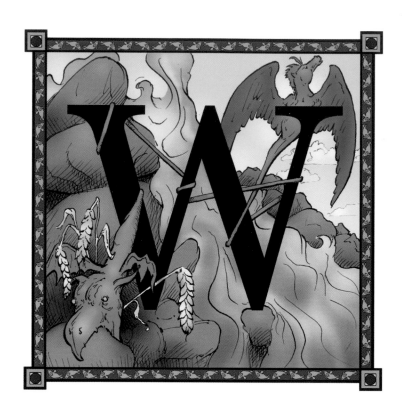

The Vólle is a mammal who
will likely start to trouble you
because he lacks a W,
but if you had a second head
that also needed to be fed
and fought you when it's time for bed,
why would it be a thing untrue
to say you were a double you?
And so the Vólle's tail permits
a double V where usually sits
a W that one admits
looks made of misnamed alpha-bits.
For W seems made of these:
not double U's, but V's!

## A Differing Tale in Sonnet Form

Whoever severs fairest Vólle's tail
Will be forever headsman of the worm,
Which turns within the heart of vale,
Or wood or cave. To end its beastly term,
One must, if able, raise an axe of fire.
O let that courser of the air ascend!
Let such a magicked steed fulfill desire
And lift on wings not fit for lesser ends.
Except if one there is whose heart gives heat,
Enough to take delight in fallen things,
Loving the lost with healing fire replete,
Or raising by degrees the worm's cold wings.
Vólle! O Vólle! You are Double here:
Evince a will to love as One draws near.

Xerona alnadae

Xerus inauris

Xenopus laevis

Xiphias gladius

# The Xero

*(...eludes the Dally and the Blug)*

Discovered by scholars in faraway vales,

The Xeros are found riding updrafts and gales.

Through the thin mountain air the Xeros career,

This way and that in       winds they can't steer.

They're light as a feather,       and the color of weather,

So a census of Xeros       was never endeavored:

Though the hill people swear there are many around,

Never—no, not ever—will Xeros go near

those who count what they've found.

The Y-It

Sometimes Y-It shows
there's nothing worse,
Than too much of
you in verse

## The Zealion

*(...sings to the dancing Dally)*

A through Z has finally,
Artfully, brought you to me!
Being, as I am, a Zealion free,
Being, as I am, at liberty,
Could I, my friends, Dally and Blug,
Convince you to give me a brotherly hug?

Don't look surprised that I call you my brothers,
Despite the fact that we have different mothers.
Even so, mammals are mammals for good reason:
(Enjoy the winter and spring? They're both seasons!)
Friends, we are all warm and furry and kind,
Feeding our young as nature designed.

Good, good! I'm so pleased that you see we're all fellows.
Gallants are grand, and the Plea loves his bellows.

Hai-chus are brave, and Nólles are sad.
Have you not noticed that some beasts are bad?
I hoped you'd also understood:
Ironically, even the bad beasts are good!

Jargontalkies are wordy but gifted.
Just as the Urnaz's chin's nobly lifted!
Keep clear of Colvaino's perilous spires,
Known to have kindled the Muses' fires!
Lundregun's hunger is natural desire.
(Alas, it's gone a little haywire.)

My goodness gracious, listen to me!
My sharp-eyed friends, do you see what I see?
Mammals will mix, like sweetness with sour,
Mix in our hearts like the fragrance of flowers.
Merely wish we be one, and it's touchingly done!

Now that you know we've kinship great,
Never forget that we've no cause to hate.
O mammals! Be the best of friends!
O wish for each other the noblest ends!
Perhaps you pitiable mammals forgot the
Preserving power that loving hath wrought?

Quite so, and what's more, you should love like me!
Quickening your hearts more zealously!
Repeat, if you wish, the Zealion's song.
Really, I promise, it's not very long:
"So what, if loving each other takes work!
Somebody else play the role of the jerk!"
Thankfully, mammals are meant to love things.
Thankfully, mammals can smile through the stings.
Unfortunately, mammals can choose to be weepy,

Unloving, uncaring, and generally sleepy.
Victory over the Evol at heart?
Victory needs good friends and good art.

Width and depth and breadth and heights,
—With them and with wisdom's sight,
Excel beyond just doing right,
Exceed the confines of the night!
You might, when there's no clear sunlight,
Yet still forget the moon is bright:
Zealous, the sun has found a way,
Zealous to bring through night the day.

# An Amusing Assortment of Additional Appendices

# A Glossary
## for *M¹r. M²ehan's M³ildly Amusing M⁴ythical M⁵ammals*
## (or *M5*, for short)

## A Note to All Children Readers about the Glossary

We all love mammals, but zoology is tough. "Children" readers may well be rebuffed. I suggest you try your best to become a grown-up here. Doing so will help you through a glossary you fear. Now. When you're ready, hold the book steady, drop your eyes from here, then read the note that's deeply true, the one to All Adult Readers, which you thought perhaps was not addressed to you?

## A Note to All Adult Readers
### *(The Fine Print)*

Some words are hard or difficult, and not knowing them can make you feel dumb, or like a dolt. What's a "dolt," you say? Don't ask me. Just look it up in the glossary. If a gloss begins with [WEB], then it comes mostly from an old cobwebbed edition of Webster's Revised Unabridged Dictionary. If the gloss begins with [DJD], then it comes more or less from the great and ancient Dr. Johnson's Dictionary. And if the gloss has [M5] at its start, then it comes mostly from Mr. Mehan's mythical arts, which means the gloss's grace is that it comes from many times and places! The [WEB] and [DJD] are true like eggs, or the time, or whether two words can rhyme. [M5] is true like a sunset, or a duet, or whether two friends are true friends yet.

# A

**account**—[DJD] 1. explanation; assignment of causes. 2. a narrative, relation.

[M5] perhaps from the Latin *comptor*, meaning one who adorns something ornately, orderly, properly embellishing it with beauty. There's much more to "account" than the counting of things, since counting is only a part of that ordering art that makes us confess that a thing is beautifully arranged.

**acquired**—[DJD] gained by one's self, in opposition to those things which are bestowed by nature; from the Latin *acquiro*, meaning to get or add to.

[M5] how strange that we mammals can put effort into gaining things that make us happy but even things that make us sad.

**additional**—[DJD] that which is added. The poet-playwright-politician Joseph Addison used the word this way: "The greatest wits, that ever were produced in one age, lived together in so good an understanding, and celebrated one another with so much generosity, that each of them receives an additional luster from his contemporaries."

**agape**—[DJD] staring with eagerness, as a bird gapes for meat.

[M5] there is also a Greek word for Love that looks just like "agape," but it does not rhyme with our Evol "ape." The Greek word is pronounced ah-GAH-peh, and originally meant something a bit more than "brotherly love." It was said about the kind of brothers that would die to save each other. Such a love is truly a wonder, so it's worth saying "AH-" at the start of "agape."

**age**—[WEB] a great period in the history of the Earth. Note: the geologic ages are as follows: 1. the Archæan, including the time when there was no life and the time of the earliest and simplest forms of life. 2. the age of Invertebrates, or the Silurian, when the life on the globe consisted distinctively of invertebrates. 3. the age of Fishes, or the Devonian, when fishes were the dominant race. 4. the age of Coal Plants, or Acrogens, or the Carboniferous age. 5. the Mesozoic or Secondary age, or age of Reptiles, when reptiles prevailed in great numbers and of vast size. 6. the Tertiary age, or age of Mammals, when the mammalia, or quadrupeds, abounded, and were the dominant race. 7. the Quaternary age, or age of Man, or the modern era.

[DJD] 1. the latter part of life; old-age; oldness. 2. any period of time attributed to something as a whole, or part, of its duration: in this sense, we say, the age of man, several ages of the world, the Golden or iron age. As the mighty poet John Milton says in *Paradise Lost*: "Destin'd Restorer of mankind, by whom / New heav'n, and earth, shall to the ages rise, / Or down from heav'n descend."

[M5] ah, the mythical Golden Age, of which the Roman poet Ovid wrote so well, was a mythical age both before the four seasons and human toil, which came in the Silver Age, and before deceit and war, which came in the Bronze Age.

**ah**—[WEB] an exclamation, expressive

of surprise, pity, complaint, entreaty, contempt, threatening, delight, triumph, etc., according to the manner of utterance.

[M5] if we can say "ah" and mean "surprise, pity, complaint, entreaty, contempt, threatening, delight, triumph, etc.," why then we'd best attend to whichever sense is meant behind whatever word is said. Ah, words, those signs of things unseen! As the poet Shakespeare wrote, "Why, saw you any thing more wonderful?"

**alas**—[WEB] an exclamation expressive of sorrow, pity, or apprehension of evil. It combines "ah-" with the Latin *lassum*, which means weary.

[M5] ah, can you see? The very word teaches you and me, that grief, sorrow, and pity can make a mammal all too weary. The word "ah" combined with that old Latin *lassum* helps us know just what sort of "ah" is meant: ah-lassum; ah-lass; ahlas; alas! "Alas" is, alas, a more complicated word than "ah," but since "ah" can mean so many things, a little complexity can help us see the meaning and sense. How funny that complexity, put forth in charity, can help us to simplicity!

**alphabetical**—[M5] having to do with the alphabet, a word made up of the first two letters of the Greek alphabet: alpha- and -beta.

**amusing**—[WEB] giving amusement; diverting; as, an amusing story.

[M5] the amusing poet Alexander Pope wrote letters to his dear friend, the portrait painter Charles Jervas, who once tried to teach Pope painting: "I thank you for your good offices, which are numberless. . . . I have the greatest proof in nature at present of the amusing power of poetry, for it takes me up so entirely, that I scarce see what passes under my nose, and hear nothing that is said about me"; and "I am just

entered upon the old way of life again, sleep and musing. It is my employment to revive the old of past ages to the present, as it is yours to transmit the young of the present to the future." Some think "amusing" comes from the Latin *musso*, meaning to be afraid to say anything out of uncertainty or fear, but while amusing things can make us hesitate or second guess what we thought was surely true, I like to think the word comes from the Muses, listed in the glossary below.

**Ango**—[M5] the blessedly shortened name for the Angogrobugunkalungstis; sounds like "mango."

**appendices**—[WEB] plural of appendix, which, among other things, means any literary matter added to a book, but not necessarily essential to its completeness, and thus distinguished from supplement, which is intended to supply deficiencies and correct inaccuracies.

[M5] I have nothing necessary or essential to add to that.

**applied**—[WEB] past tense of "apply," which means to lay or place; to put or adjust (one thing to another); to apply medicines.

[M5] one question: how could monster fuzz be applied as a medicine?

**arsis**—[WEB] in poetry, that part of a metrical foot that is distinguished from the rest (known as the thesis) of the foot by a greater stress of voice. (b) That elevation of voice now called metrical accentuation, or the rhythmic accent.

[M5] syllables are a key part of poetry's rhythm. For instance, the proper way to say "arsis" is to stress the first syllable, so the arsis of "arsis" is the "ARE" in "ARE-sis." Syllables, those little parts of longer words, are either stressed or unstressed. "ARE" is stressed; "-sis" is unstressed. (Try stressing the wrong syllable: "are-SIS.") These stresses in words make

English poetry have a beat, a rhythm, a meter. Listen: "aMONG the PELTing DROPS of RAIN, / the DALLy CAN be SEEN aGAIN"—daDUM daDUM daDUM daDUM / daDUM daDUM daDUM daDUM. The DUM in daDUM—the DUM arsis.

**ascendant**—[WEB] 1. rising toward the zenith; above the horizon. 2. rising; ascending. 3. superior; surpassing; ruling. Consider the English historian George Grote: "Without some power of persuading or confuting, of defending himself against accusations . . . no man could possibly hold an ascendant position."

**aseptic**—[WEB] not liable to putrefaction; nonputrescent.

**ashore**—[WEB] on shore or on land.

**asp**—[WEB] a small, hooded, poisonous serpent of Egypt and adjacent countries, whose bite is often fatal.

[M5] oddly enough, according the ancient *Dictionary of English Plant Names*, asp is also a name for any kind of poplar tree or specifically the *Populus tremula*. More freely, the Latin *populus* can also mean a people or citizens, who should never be tremulous, which means shaking, affected with fear.

**assizer**—[WEB] 1. an officer who has the care or inspection of weights and measures, etc. 2. a knight or some very substantial man who sits in judgment, as on a jury.

**assortment**—[DJD] an arrangement into classes, as one thing suits with another.

**assotting**—[WEB] besotting, befooling, beguiling, infatuating. As the high-poet Spenser's poetry has it: "Willie, I ween [or reckon that] thou be assot"; and "Some ecstasy assotted had his sense." (The word is obsolete and hardly used.)

[M5] perhaps the Urnaz is so popular that people foolishly lose their heads just speaking about him!

**assumental**—[WEB] an "assument" means a patch; an addition; a piece put on.

[M5] so this new word "assumental" could mean anything to do with an addition.

**asteism**—[WEB] genteel irony; a polite and ingenious manner of deriding another.

[M5] "genteel" means polite, elegant in behavior, civil; "irony" means saying things in a clever, roundabout way, as in the poetess Emily Dickinson's wise poem, "Tell All the Truth but Tell it Slant"; and "ingenuous" comes from the Latin *ingenuus*, meaning noble, frank, upright, candid, and like a free person, and also from other, similar, clever Latin words.

**asterism**—[WEB] 1. a constellation, a small cluster of stars. 2. an asterisk, three asterisks placed in this manner (*\*\**) to direct attention to a particular passage. 3. an optical property of some crystals which exhibit a star-shape by reflected light, as a star sapphire, or by transmitted light, as some mica.

**astheny**—[WEB] want or loss of strength; debility; diminution of the vital forces.

[M5] perhaps the people praising the Urnaz mean that they grow weak in praising him so much? Or that the Urnaz is their one weakness? Like chocolate or some other dessert that's hard to resist?

**astonishing**—[WEB] very wonderful; of a nature to excite astonishment; as an astonishing event.

**astral**—[WEB] 1. starry; starlike. 2. astral spirits, spirits formerly supposed to live in the heavenly bodies or the aërial regions, and represented in the Middle Ages as fallen angels, spirits of the dead, or spirits originating in fire.

**astrogeny**—[WEB] the creation or evolution of the stars or the heavens.

**awe**—[DJD] reverential fear; reverence.
[WEB] 1. dread; great fear mingled with respect. As the august poet

86

William Cowper wrote of the mythic schoolmaster and sage called Discipline, "His frown was full of terror, and his voice Shook the delinquent with such fits of awe."

**awful**—[DJD] 1. that which strikes with awe, or fills with reverence. 2. worshipful; in authority; invested with dignity. This sense is obsolete.

[WEB] frightful; exceedingly bad; great; oppressing with fear or horror; appalling; terrible; as, an awful scene.

# B

**beast**—[WEB] 1. any living creature; an animal, including man, insects, etc. 2. any four-footed animal, that may be used for labor, food, or sport; as, a beast of burden. "A just man regardeth the life of his beast" (Prv 12:10).

[DJD] 1. an animal distinguished from birds, insects, fishes, and man. 2. an irrational animal, opposed to man; as "man and beast." 3. a brutal, savage man; a man acting in any manner unworthy of a reasonable creature.

**beautiful**—[DJD] fair, having the qualities that constitute beauty, which is that assemblage of graces, or proportion of parts which pleases the eye or that particular grace, feature, or ornament.

As the English poet-diplomat Matthew Prior wrote, "Beautiful looks are ruled by fickle minds, / And summer seas are turned by sudden winds."

**beckons**—[WEB] to make a significant sign to; hence, to summon, as by a motion of the hand.

**befouling**—[DJD] to make foul; to soil; to dirty.

[WEB] to entangle or run against so as to impede motion.

**behave**—[WEB] to carry; to conduct; to comport; to manage; to bear.

[M5] we get the word "conduct" from the Latin *con-* meaning with and *-ductus* meaning command. When we truly behave ourselves, we do so with command over ourselves.

**behold**—[WEB] to have in sight; to see clearly; to look at; to regard with the eyes.

[DJD] an interjection meaning see, lo; a word by which attention is excited, or admiration noted. "Behold! I am with thee, and will keep thee" (Gn 28:15).

**bellows**—[DJD] 1. to make a noise as a bull, a violent outcry; to clamor; to roar as the sea in a storm, or as a wind; of human beings: loud deep cries or roars. 2. the instrument used to blow the fire. Metaphorically, the poet-statesman Sir Philip Sidney wrote, "Since sighs into my inward furnace turned, / For bellows serve to kindle more the fire."

**besot**—[DJD] to infatuate, to stupefy, to dull, to take away the senses. As the preacher Robert South brusquely put it, "He is besotted, and has lost his reason; and what then can there be for religion to take hold of him by?"

**bested**—[WEB] past tense of the verb "to best," meaning to get the better of.

**beware**—[DJD] to regard with caution; to be suspicious of danger from someone or something.

**billion**—[WEB] a thousand millions, or 1,000,000,000.

[M5] a word we use to describe numbers beyond our unaided human power to count. To count to one billion would take a lifetime, assuming you never lost count!

**birch**—[WEB] 1. a tree of several species, constituting the genus *Betula*; as, the white or common birch (*Betula alba*) (also called the silver birch or lady birch); the dwarf birch (*Betula glandulosa*); the paper or canoe birch (*Betula papyracea*); the yellow birch (*Betula lutea*); and the black or cherry birch (*Betula lenta*). Other species include the dwarf birch (*Betula nana*) and the drooping birch (*Betula pendula*). 2. to whip with a birch rod or twig; to flog.

[DJD] Dr. Johnson reminds us that the birch's leaves are like those of the poplar; the shoots are very slender and weak; and the seeds are winged. And that it delights in poor soil.

[M5] the yellow or golden birch (*Betula lutea*) can sometimes cross with a paper birch, and that beautiful, rare kind of hybrid golden birch, which is only found wrapped and hidden in the deepest and oldest woods, glimmers at night in the crackling torchlight, like flecks of gold and ivory, much the way sand and water shimmer in the sunlight or the way a woodland creature's eyes might flash in the light of the moon. It is this very special kind of golden birch that the Gallant befriended, which, if I may, I'd like to name the sandy birch (*Betula harenosa*).

**blossom**—[DJD] 1. the flower that grows on any plant; we generally call those flowers blossoms, which are not much regarded in themselves, but as token of some following production. 2. to put forth blossoms.

[M5] a blossom is often a sign or "token" of spring and hopefulness, in part because a blossom pops out new life where all seemed lifeless.

**blubber**—[WEB] 1. the fat of whales and other large sea animals from which oil is obtained. It lies immediately under the skin and over the muscular flesh. 2. to weep noisily, or so as to disfigure the face; to cry in a childish manner.

**blubberous**—[M5] a rare word usually having to do with weeping, but nothing stops us from adding another sense of the word, namely the sense of being quite fat and full of blubber, like a whale.

**Blueberry Hill**—[M5] while there are many places with this same, common name, this very real hill is one uncommonly special to me—too special to describe in a glossary; I hope you have a special place in the woods where your heart and you can go now and again.

**Blug**—[M5] this mythical mammal's name rhymes with "slug," but I already told you that in the poem, if you listened to the rhyme and rhythm.

**boughs**—[DJD] plural of "bough," meaning an arm or large shoot of a tree, bigger than a branch, yet not always distinguished from it.

[M5] rhymes with "vows."

**breadth**—[DJD] 1. the distance from side to side of any surface or thing. 2. regarding the fine arts, the quality of having the colors and shadows broad and massive, and the arrangement of objects such as to avoid a great multiplicity of details, producing an impression of largeness and simple grandeur; called also breadth of effect.

[M5] avoiding a "great multiplicity" means giving thought and way to the whole of something, which, as we all know, is never merely the sum of that something's many parts. If you were only the sum of your parts, simply added together, why then, you'd stop being you if you got a haircut and a mouse would not be a mouse if the butcher's wife cut off its tail! Thank God that none of us mammals is a mere addition problem! Nobody said a painting or a poem was beautiful because it was a pile of parts. No. It's beautiful because it's one whole—one beautiful thing—a work of art with "simple grandeur."

**bristles**—[WEB] to rise or stand erect, like bristles.

**broil**—[DJD] 1. to be in the heat. 2. to dress or cook by laying on the coals, or before the fire. 3. a tumult; a quarrel, as, for instance, Shakespeare wrote of civil war-torn Scotland in *Macbeth*: "Say to the king the knowledge of the broil, /As thou didst leave it."

**brusquely**—[WEB] roughly and promptly in manner; bluntly; abruptly.

**buffalo**—[WEB] any species of wild ox; a name for the bison of North America.
   [M5] I prefer using "buffalo" for "the bison of North America" like I prefer using "Ango" for "Angogrobugunkalungstis."

**bulbous**—[WEB] having or containing bulbs, or a bulb; growing from bulbs; bulblike in shape or structure.

**bulk**—[WEB] 1. magnitude of material substance; dimensions; mass; size; as, an ox or ship of great bulk. 2. the main mass or body; the largest or principal portion; the majority. 3. the body, with the sense of size, magnitude, dimension, volume, bigness, largeness, or massiveness. 4. the cargo of a vessel when stowed.

**bull**—[WEB] the male of any species of cattle (*Bovidæ*); hence, the male of any large quadruped, as the elephant; also any male whale.
   [DJD] 1. the male to a cow. 2. a blunder; a contradiction. 3. as a prefix,

"bull-" generally notes the large size of anything.

**bumbling**—[WEB] 1. making a hollow or humming noise, like that of the bumblebee; calling like the low and curious call of the bittern, a marsh bird. The poet and civil servant Geoffrey Chaucer, in his *Canterbury Tales*, put it just so: "And as a bittern bumbleth in the mire."

# C

**candor**—[DJD] sweetness of temper; purity of mind; openness; ingenuity; kindness.
   [WEB] whiteness; brightness; (as applied to moral conditions) unsullied purity; innocence.
   [M5] candor means letting the truth you know shine forth in what you do and say, without the stain of deceit. The Declaration of Independence of the United States of America uses candor in defense of civic liberty against tyranny: "To prove this, let Facts be submitted to a candid world." In the Roman orator Cicero's *De Republica* or *Republic*, the Latin word *candor*, meaning dazzling clarity or brightness, describes the stars of heaven in "Scipio's Dream": "Follow the examples of your grandfather here, and of me, your father, in paying a strict regard to justice [*iustitiam*] and piety [*pietatem*], greatly towards parents and relations, and then greatest of all toward your country [*patria*]. Such a life as this is the true way to heaven, and to the company of those, who, after having lived on earth

and shed the body, inhabit the place you now see: this was the shining circle whose remarkable brightness [*candor*] distinguishes it among the constellations, and which after the Greeks you call the Milky Way [*orbem lacteum*]."

**canopy**—[DJD] 1. a covering of state over a throne or bed; a covering spread over the head. As the refined poet John Dryden wrote, "The birch, the myrtle, and the bay, / Like friends did all embrace; And their large branches did display, / To canopy the place."

**career**—[DJD] 1. the ground on which a race is run, a course, a race. 2. full speed; swift motion. 3. course of action; uninterrupted procedure. 4. to run with swift motion.

**cause**—[DJD] 1. from the Latin *causa*, that which produces or effects any thing; the efficient. 2. the reason; motive to any thing. 3. side; party; ground or principle of action or opposition; as civil servant and poet Thomas Tickell put it, "Ere to thy cause, and thee, my heart inclin'd, / Or love to party had seduced my mind."

   [M5] much of what makes one wise is the knowledge of causes, especially knowledge of the Cause of all causes and the knowledge of which causes are worth striving for and how.

**caving**—[M5] the simpler way of saying spelunking, which is the fancier way of saying fiddling about in caves or, well, caving.

**census**—[WEB] an official registration of the number of the people, the value of their estates, and other general statistics of a country. Note: a general census of the United States was first taken in 1790, and one has been taken at the end of every ten years since.

**cicadas**—[M5] maybe you've heard these flying insects whirring and buzzing on a hot summer's day, or maybe you've lived through one of the great

brood hatches of the thirteen-year or seventeen-year cicadas, called *Magicicada septendecim* (which is Latin for the great cicada seventeen). In a brood hatch, billions of cicadas crawl out of the ground and into the trees, after seventeen years in the earth. In the philosopher Plato's famous dialogue the *Phaedrus*, the wise man Socrates tells the myth of the cicadas: they were people who, once the Muses and singing were brought into the world, never ceased in the pleasures of song. They were so taken by love of song that they forgot to eat or drink, and so they died of singing. Later these people came back as cicadas, honored by the Muses simply to chirp and sing without having to eat or drink, which is just how cicadas live in the trees to this day. While cicadas do, in fact, drink sap, they can still sing as they drink, for their song comes from tymbals, special organs in their abdomens just for singing! To sing without ceasing? No wonder their scientific name is *Magicicada*! See the entry for "Muses" below.

**civil**—[DJD] 1. relating to the community; political; relating to the city or government. 2. not in anarchy, not wild, not without rule or government. 3. civilized, not barbarous; gentle, elegant of manners, not brutal, rude, or coarse. 4. not concerning ecclesial, military, foreign, or criminal matters.

   [M5] the quality of kind and charitable regard that one person has for another and that leads to peace and friendship, which can only be fostered in a loving, not a fearful, setting.

**Colvaino**—[M5] this mythical mammal sounds like "coal," "vein," and "oh" all forged together: coal-VEIN-oh—Colvaino.

**common**—[DJD] belonging equally to more than one; public, general; serving the use of all; frequent, usual, ordinary.

"Though life and sense be common to man and brutes, and their operations in many things alike; yet by this form he lives the life of a man, and not of a brute, and hath the sense of a man, and not of a brute" (Hale's *Origin of Mankind*).

compare—[DJD] 1. to make one thing the measure of another; to estimate the relative goodness or badness, or other qualities, of any one thing, but observing how it differs from something else. 2. it may be observed, that when the comparison intends only similitude or illustration of likeness, we use "to" before the thing brought for illustration; as, "he compared anger to fire." Likewise, when two persons or things are compared, to discover their relative proportion of any quality, "with" is used before the thing used as the measure: "Black Macbeth / Will seem as pure as snow, being compared / With my confineless harms" (Shakespeare's *Macbeth*).

concaves—[DJD] a hollow without angles; as, the inner surface of an eggshell, the inner curve of an arch: opposed to convex. "Have you not made an universal shout, / That Tyber trembled underneath his banks, / To hear the replication of your sounds, / Made in his concave shores?" (Shakespeare's *Julius Caesar*).

conceal—[DJD] to hide, to keep secret; not to divulge; to cover. Also, Broome's *Notes on the Odyssey* wisely offers a point concerning this ancient Greek, Homeric hero and his prudence of holding his tongue: "Ulysses himself adds, he was the most eloquent and the most silent of men: he knew that a word spoke never wrought so much good as a word concealed."

[M5] N. B. (short for *nota bene* and Italian for note well) to conceal something is not necessarily to lie. Lying is telling someone something that's false; concealing is holding something back, perhaps until later, when that someone is ready to hear or see that something concealed.

congealed—[DJD] turned, by frost, from a fluid to a solid state; bound or fixed, as by cold.

considerable—[DJD] 1. worthy of consideration; worthy of regard or attention. 2. respectable; above neglect; deserving notice. 3. more than a little, less than a great deal. 4. important, valuable. The refined poet John Dryden: "In painting, not every action nor every person is considerable enough to enter into the cloth."

convince—[DJD] to force another to acknowledge a contested position; to overpower, surmount. 2. to convict; to prove guilty of. 3. to evince; to prove; to manifest; to vindicate. It comes from the Latin root words of *vincere*, meaning conquer, and *con-*, meaning (in this case) with, together.

[M5] so if you con-vince someone of some truth, the Latin implies that the two (or three? or more?) of you have conquered together either ignorance or lies or both!

coomb—[WEB] 1. a hollow in a hillside. 2. the unwatered portion of a valley which forms its continuation beyond and above the most elevated spring that issues into it.

corpulent—[DJD] 1. fleshy; bulky; having great bodily bulk. As the poet and playwright Ben Jonson wrote in his *Discoveries Made upon Men and Matter*, "We say it is a fleshy style, when there is much periphrases and circuit of words; and when with more than enough, it grows fat and corpulent."

[M5] periphrasis (the singular of periphrases) is the rhetorical trick— or mental and verbal tick!—of saying things in a needlessly complicated way, using elaborate and extraneous complexity in a manner unnecessary, speaking around the thing you mean either because you do not actually know what you mean or because what you know is, in truth, fairly simple and unexciting if you were to communicate it simply and straightforwardly or because you simply love to hear yourself talk in a way or manner that is replete with not very needful complexity. When done well, periphrasis is beautiful, or great and full of beauty.

**courser**—[WEB] 1. one who courses or hunts. 2. a swift or spirited horse; a racer or war horse; a charger.

**cow**—[DJD] 1. the female of the bull. 2. the horned female animal with cloven feet, kept for her milk and calves.

**creature**—[DJD] 1. a being not self-existent, but created by the supreme power. 2. anything created. 3. an animal not human. 4. a general term for man. 5. a word of contempt for a human. 6. a word of petty tenderness. 7. a person who owes his rise or his fortune to another.

**crown**—[DJD] 1. the ornament of the head which denotes imperial or royal dignity. 2. a garland. 3. reward; honorary distinction. 5. the top of the head. 6. the top of anything, as John Dryden translates Virgil's great Roman epic, the *Aeneid*, when the Trojans cut ancient and sacred trees for their ships, "Huge trunks of trees, felled from the steepy crown / Of the bare mountains, roll with ruin down."

**cumbersome**—[DJD] troublesome, vexatious; burdensome; embarrassing; unwieldy, unmanageable.

**curlicue**—[M5] amazing curls. On a paper birch or on that special kind of golden birch-paper birch crossbreed, which we can call the sandy birch, such curlicues look like the rolled up ends of ancient scrolls, as if you could peal back that fantastically twisted bark and read the history of the forest. See the entry for "birch" above.

# D

**dabbed**—[DJD] past tense of "dab," to strike gently with something soft or moist.

    [WEB] to strike by a thrust; to hit with a sudden blow or thrust. Sir Thomas More wrote, "And St. Paul himself confesses, that for a medicinal preservative against pride, there was given to him the angel Satan, the prick of the flesh, to dab him in the neck and make him stop and beat him."

**dainty**—[DJD] 1. something nice or delicate; something of exquisite taste; an old word of fondness: "Why, that's my dainty; I shall miss thee: / But yet thou shalt have freedom" (Shakespeare's *Tempest*). 2. pleasing to the palate; of exquisite taste; delicate; of acute sensibility; nice; soft; tender; scrupulous; ceremonious; elegant; tenderly, languishingly, or effeminately beautiful.

**dally**—[DJD] to sport, to play, to frolic; to trifle, to play the fool, to amuse one's self with idle play, to lose time in trifles. In Shakespeare's tragedy *King Lear*, the Earl of Gloucester, to save the distracted and nearly mad King Lear from a murderous plot, exhorts the Earl of Kent: "If thou shouldst dally half an hour, his life, / With thine, and all that offer to defend him, / Stand in assured loss. Take up, take up! / And follow me, that will to some provision / Give thee quick conduct."

[WEB] to delay unnecessarily; to while away.

**Dally**—[M5] you say "Dally" like "valley," but with a "D"; and while usually dry, the Dally can, alas, become quite dabby, which comes from "dabble" which means to play in water or move in water or mud. A dabby thing is wet and muddy. It is impossible for you to see a dabby Dally dancing dry.

**dancing**—[M5] when the mind, the heart, and the body move as one in the joy of that very unity and in the rhythm of the heavens. For anything less than that, see "flail" below.

**death**—[M5] one of the wisest and best definitions of death comes from Socrates: death is the separation of the body from the soul. Of course, he was speaking of us humans, with our immortal souls, which will never cease to be. Amazing to think that if you can read this, you will never not be!

**deign**—[DJD] 1. to grant; to permit; to allow. 2. to vouchsafe; to think worthy. As the amusing Alexander Pope wrote, "Oh deign to visit our forsaken seats, / The mossy fountains, and the green retreats."

[M5] the great and good know it is worthy to help in some way those beneath them, because love always weighs our similarities more favorably in the balance, and our differences more lightly.

**delight**—[DJD] 1. joy, content, satisfaction; that which gives delight. 2. to please, to content, to satisfy, to afford pleasure. As King David sings in the Book of Psalms, "Delight in the Lord, and he will give thee the requests of thy heart."

**desire**—[DJD] 1. wish; eagerness to obtain or enjoy; from the Latin *desiderium*.

[M5] that Latin word, *desiderium*,

means a strong desire of the heart as yet unfulfilled. Perhaps it comes from *de-* and *-sido*, together meaning of sitting. We must sit and foster a wish or desire, but we often sit too long with a desire, and delaying so may fill us with regret, which is another meaning of *desiderium*. Rather, we ought to be up and after it with desire, with *desiderium*!

That Latin word is the first name of the famous Christian Humanist Desiderius Erasmus (yes, that's his real first name!). Consider this advice on desire from that old Latin and Greek scholar, in a book Erasmus wrote on the education of young leaders: "Go unto the way of life, not slothfully, not fearfully: but with sure purpose, with all thy heart, with a confident mind, and (if I may say so) with such a mind as . . . would rather fight than drink: so that thou be ready at all hours for Christ's sake to lose both life and goods. A slothful man will and will not." Become a man or woman of real desire, as Desiderius suggests.

Desiderius Erasmus also wrote *In Praise of Folley*, which in Latin was originally called *Moriae Encomium*, jokingly named for his dear friend, another great Christian Humanist, Thomas More. Any sort of truly human humanism, but especially Christian Humanism, fosters a deep desire for sure and loving friendship!

**despair**—[DJD] hopelessness; despondence; loss of hope; in theology, it is the loss of confidence in the mercy of God.

[M5] despair is always a mistake because the despairing mind pretends darkly to know what it can never know, namely all that the future holds.

**despite**—[DJD] 1. malice, anger, malignity, maliciousness, spleen, hatred. As Shakespeare wrote in his play *Coriolanus*, about the ancient Roman republic and the dangers of pride to a people, "Thou wretch! Despite o'erwhelm thee!" 2. defiance.

[M5] the word may combine "des-," meaning without or not, and "pity": despite is to be without proper pity for others.

**digits**—[WEB] 1. a finger or toe. 2. one of the ten figures or symbols, 0, 1, 2, 3, 4, 5, as well as 6, 7, 8, and 9, by which all numbers are expressed—so called because of the use of fingers (or toes!) in counting and computing. 3. one twelfth part of the diameter of the sun or moon; a term used to express the quantity of an eclipse.

**disbelieve**—[DJD] not to credit, not to hold as true. "Our belief or disbelief of a thing does not alter the nature of the thing" (Tillotson's *Sermons*).

[M5] it is funny to notice that, in Roman mythology, Dis is the ancient mythological underworld and kingdom of Pluto, god of the dead, and that adding "dis-" to the word "believe" leaves one subject to such lower kings.

**displays**—[DJD] 1. to exhibit to the sight or mind. 2. to talk without restraint; to set ostentatiously to view. 3. exhibitions of anything to view.

**distinctly**—[DJD] plainly, clearly.

**dodgy**—[M5] possessing the quality of skillful movement, evasion, hence, by extension, skillfull in witty stratagems and concealments.

**dolorous**—[DJD] 1. sorrowful, doleful, dismal, gloomy. "You take me in too dolorous a sense; / I spake t'you for your comfort" (Shakespeare's *Antony and Cleopatra*).

**dolt**—[DJD] 1. a heavy, stupid fellow; a blockhead; a thicksoul; a loggerhead.

**droves**—[DJD] numbers of cattle, sheep, or any herds of oxen that may be managed by any noise or cry which the drivers shall accustom them to; any collection of animals; a crowd, a tumult.

**dunces**—[DJD] a dunce is a dullard, a dolt, a thickskull; a stupid, indocile animal.

[M5] a dunce has knowledge but no wit how to use it.

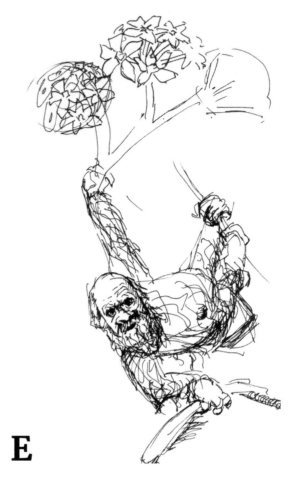

# E

**eddy**—[DJD] the water that by some repercussion, or opposite wind, runs contrary to the main stream; a whirlpool; circular motion.

**elephant**—[M5] the ancient Roman naturalist Pliny the Elder declared this noblest mammal "the first of all the land animals." He continued, "The elephant is the largest of them all, and in intelligence approaches the nearest to man. It understands the language of its country, it obeys commands, and it remembers all the duties which it has been taught. It is sensible alike of the pleasures of love and glory, and, to a degree that is rare among men even, possesses notions of honesty, prudence, and equity; it has a religious respect also for the stars, and a veneration for the sun and the moon." Quite a creature! Pliny says much more about the elephant, and he shows especially how concerned they are for each other. The poet John Gay, whose beast fables contain an elephant, one smarter than a bookseller (and able to read ancient Greek!), wrote this in praise of the elephant:

Who doubts that elephants are found
For science and for sense renowned?
Borri records their strength of parts,
Extent of thought, and skill in arts;
How they perform the law's decrees,
And save the state the hangman's fees;
And how by travel understand
The language of another land.
Let those, who question this report,
To Pliny's ancient page resort;

While we may "question this report," Pliny's description speaks real truth, of a sort. In any case, it seems there's far more to elephants than the way they smell. Don't let your nose fool you!

**endeavored**—[DJD] the past tense of "endeavor," meaning to attempt; to try; to labor to a certain purpose; to work for a certain end.

[M5] for example, in his Epistle 5, the Roman statesman-poet Seneca writes to his young friend Lucilius: "I commend you and rejoice in the fact that you are persistent in your studies, and that, putting all else aside, you make it each day your endeavor to become a better man." While not a perfect book, Seneca's *Epistles* may be the greatest work ever written by a pagan. St. Jerome thought so; he thought it was the one pagan book every Christian—and anyone who wants a life of virtue—should endeavor to read.

**enjoy**—[DJD] to feel or perceive with pleasure; to have a pleasing sense of; to be delighted with. As the poet and politician Joseph Addison had the mighty and strict Roman philosopher-statesman Cato say, "I could enjoy the pangs of death, / And smile in agony"

(Addison's *Cato, A Tragedy*).

[M5] Augustine of Hippo (the city, not the mammal!) said this of enjoyment: "There are some things, then, which are to be enjoyed, others which are to be used, others still which we enjoy and use. Those things which are objects of enjoyment make us happy. Those things which are objects of use assist, and (so to speak) support us in our efforts after happiness, so that we can attain the things that make us happy and rest in them. . . . Suppose, then, we were wanderers in a strange country, and could not live happily away from our fatherland, and that we felt wretched in our wandering, and wishing to put an end to our misery, determined to return home. We find, however, that we must make use of some mode of conveyance, either by land or water, in order to reach that fatherland where our enjoyment is to commence. But the beauty of the country through which we pass, and the very pleasure of the motion, charm our hearts, and turning these things, which we ought to use, into objects of enjoyment, we become unwilling to hasten the end of our journey; and becoming engrossed in an artificial delight, our thoughts are diverted from that home whose delights would make us truly happy."

**evince**—[DJD] to prove; to show; to manifest; to make evident.

**Evol**—[M5] proof that one does not need eyes to cry.

**existence**—[DJD] state of being; actual possession of being. "When a being is considered as possible, it is said to have an essence or nature: such were all things before the creation. When it is considered as actual, then it is said to have existence also" (Watt's *Logick*).

[M5] of all the mammals in existence, only humans think about being.

**expired**—[DJD] past tense of "expire,"

95

which means: 1. to exhale the last emission of breath; to die. 2. to conclude; to terminate; to come to an end.

eye—[M5] the window to the soul, but not the door to the soul.

**F**

Fáh-la-las—[M5] pronounced FA-la-la with accent on the first of three syllables, as in "animal," "heavenly," and, in a way, "Bethlehem."

fame—[DJD] 1. celebrity; renown. 2. report, rumor.

fare—[WEB] 1. the price of passage or going; the sum paid or due for conveying a person by land or water. 2. a journey; a passage. 3. bustle, business, ado.

fates—[WEB] 1. a fixed decree by which the order of things is prescribed; the immutable law of the universe; inevitable necessity; the force by which all existence is determined and conditioned. 2. appointed lot; allotted life; arranged or predetermined event; destiny; especially final lot; doom; ruin; death. 3. the three Greco-Roman goddesses, Clotho, Lachesis, and Atropos, sometimes called the Destinies, or Parcae, who were supposed to determine the course of human life. They are represented, one as holding the distaff, a second as spinning, and the third as cutting off the thread.

[DJD] 1. destiny; the eternal series of successive causes. 2. death, destruction. 3. cause of death. "The whizzing arrow sings, / And bears thy fate, Antinous, on its wings" (Alexander Pope's translation of Homer's *Odyssey*, Book 22: "The Death of the Suitors").

[M5] young and foolish Antinous was the first suitor to die at the hands of Odysseus and his son Telemachus, all for breaking the ancient rule of xenia, the universal law of hospitality, bearing on both host and, in this sorry case of the impious Antinous, ungrateful guest. The old Latin *fatum* tends to mean anything that is predicted or prophetically destined, but, as here with Antonius' death, "fate" especially means the one thing we mammals can't escape: death. The poet-statesman Thomas More composed Latin poems, a few of them about death, and he called death the *futura fata*, or future fate: "*Non ego quos rapuit mors, defleo. Defleo vivos, / Quos urunt longo fata futura metu.*" In English: "I do not weep for those whom death has snatched away, / I weep for those whom future fates do burn with lasting fear."

fen—[DJD] 1. a marsh; low flat and moist ground; a moor; a bog.

fiefdom—[WEB] an estate held of a superior on condition of military service.

[DJD] 1. a fee; a manor; a possession held by some tenure of a superior.

figuratively—[DJD] by a figure; in a sense different from that which words originally imply; not literally. The refined John Dryden, in his dedication to his translation of the greatest Roman satirist, the biting Juvenal, says this of satire: "Satire is a kind of poetry in which human vices are represented, partly dramatically, partly simply; but, for the most part, figuratively and occultly."

**filaments**—[DJD] a slender thread; a body slender and long like a thread.

**fitful**—[DJD] varied by paroxysms; disordered by a change of maladies.

[M5] if you throw a dozen fits, you'll know just what it's like to be fitful. Shakespeare's wicked King Macbeth threw many, terrible fits, as when he complained that he was alive and the king he murdered was dead: "Duncan is in his grave. / After life's fitful fever he sleeps well."

**flabby**—[DJD] soft; not firm; easily shaking or yielding to the touch.

**flail**—[M5] when you flop and flap about in the most awkward way, as though you were using a flail, which, the WEB tells us, is an instrument for threshing or beating grain or an ancient weapon with spikes on one end.

**fleece**—[DJD] as much wool as is shorn from one sheep. "Her funny locks / Hang on her temples like a golden fleece" (Shakespeare's *As You Like It*).

[M5] Shakespeare is here referring to another great myth, that of the Golden Fleece. The ancient Greek legend tells of the flying Golden Ram and the hero Jason, who, with his crew of Argonauts, sought his rightful throne by means of the ram's Golden Fleece.

**floundering**—[DJD] struggling with violent and irregular motions: as a horse in the mire.

**flub**—[M5] to make a mess of something you attempted; perhaps you flubbed your first attempt at saying "Angogrobugunkalungstis"?

**flurry**—[WEB] 1. a sudden and brief blast or gust; a light, temporary breeze. As the witty Jonathan Swift says in the wise *Gulliver's Travels*, "The boat was overset by a sudden flurry from the North." 2. a light shower or snowfall accompanied with wind. As the jovial poet Henry Wadsworth Longfellow wrote, in his lovely poem about the American pilgrims, "The Courtship of Miles Standish," "And, like a flurry of snow on the whistling wind of December, / Swift and sudden and keen came the flight of feathery arrows." 3. violent agitation; commotion; bustle; hurry. 4. the violent spasms of a dying whale.

[M5] Herman Melville describes quite a few flurries in his mighty whaling novel, *Moby Dick*: "And now abating in his flurry, the whale once more rolled out into view; surging from side to side; spasmodically dilating and contracting his spout-hole, with sharp, cracking, agonized respirations." Alas, I do not like the flurry of whales, for it seems to me too much like the passing of a life-age.

**Folley**—[M5] the last name of my dear friend and illustrator, Mr. John Folley. How important that "e" in his name must be!

**folly**—[DJD] 1. want of understanding; weakness of intellect 2. criminal weakness; depravity of mind. 3. acts of negligence or passion unbecoming gravity or deep wisdom. In this sense it has a plural: "Love is blind, and lovers cannot see / The pretty follies that themselves commit; / For if they could, Cupid himself would blush / To see me thus transformed to a boy" (Shakespeare's *Merchant of Venice*).

[M5] the ancient and famously wise King Solomon's *Proverbs* warn young men to steer clear of Lady Folly and hold tight to Lady Wisdom, who advises, "Leave childishness, and live and walk by the ways of prudence." The Latin word used for childishness is *infantiam*, which means one who cannot speak, where we get our word "infant," a baby

97

who can't yet speak. So you see, poetry, and the arts of speech generally, may help you steer clear of Lady Folly and find the prudence of Lady Wisdom. And King Solomon is not the only one who seems to think so.

**fool**—[DJD] 1. one whom nature has denied reason; a natural; an idiot. 2. in Scripture, a wicked man. "The fool sayeth in his heart there is no God" (Ps 13:1). 3. a term of indignity and reproach. 4. one who counterfeits folly; a buffoon; a jester.

[M5] that last sort of fool, my favorite kind, is the sort we all must be from time to time. For when our friends and family are heavy of heart, we mustn't be too proud to play the fool to cheer them up.

**footfalls**—[WEB] a setting down of the foot; a footstep; the sound of a footstep. The word was coined by Shakespeare.

**forgetting**—[M5] what happens when we crowd out of our mind all our memories except those we need for getting the things we should not want. It's very often a wrong we do to ourselves, which is why we have the expression, "I forgot myself" and why that saying is happily followed by "I beg your pardon," because—don't forget—when we hurt ourselves, we always hurt those we know and love.

**fragrance**—[DJD] sweetness of smell; pleasant scent; grateful odor.

[M5] smell, one of the five senses, can bring back memories deep in the mind; one whiff of a certain smell can call an old man's mind back seventy years!

**friend**—[DJD] one joined to another in mutual benevolence and intimacy.

[M5] the Roman orator Cicero, in his beautiful little book *On Friendship*, says we can learn something special about friendship—he calls it *amicitia*, from

*amor*, meaning love—by observing not-so-mythical mammals found in nature: "It seems to me that friendship springs rather from nature than from need, and from an inclination of the soul joined with a feeling of love rather than from calculation of how much profit the friendship is likely to afford. What this feeling is may be perceived even in the case of certain animals, which, up to a certain time, so love their offspring and are so loved by them, that their impulses are easily seen. But this is much more evident in man."

And when people worry too much about the profit they might get from a friend, Cicero says, "they fail to attain that loveliest, most spontaneous friendship, which is desirable in and for itself; and they do not learn from their own experience what the power of such a friendship is and are ignorant of its nature and extent. For everyone loves himself on his own account; and unless this same feeling were transferred to friendship, the real friend would never be found; for he is, as it were, another self.

"Now if it is evident in animals, whether of the air, the water, or the land, and whether tame or wild, first that they love themselves—for this feeling is born alike in every living creature—and secondly, that they require and eagerly search for other animals of their own kind to which they might attach themselves—and this they do with a longing in some degree resembling human love—than how much more, by the law of his nature, is this the case with man who both loves himself and uses his reason to seek out another whose soul he may so mingle with his own as almost to make one out of two!" I hope we all develop a knack for such wonderful friendship!

**fungi**—[M5] the plural of fungus; more commonly known as mushrooms. It sounds enough like "fun guy" to make this famously awful pun: "Why is the mushroom invited to every party? Because he's a . . . fungi!" Forgive me, but I love puns, because the only butt of such jokes is the teller. As one of the editors of Webster's Dictionary, a grammarian and schoolmaster-turned-legislator, old Professor William Chauncy Fowler tells us, the fancy Greek word for punning is *paronomasia*, which literally means *near the name*. This book has more than a few punny jokes.

**funky**—[M5] it originally meant stinky, but then it understandably came to mean fearful. Now it means weird, odd, or strangely unfamiliar, which makes sense because "to funk" used to mean panicking before some precipice or abyss—fear of the unknown. Don't be afraid of those unknown, funky words!

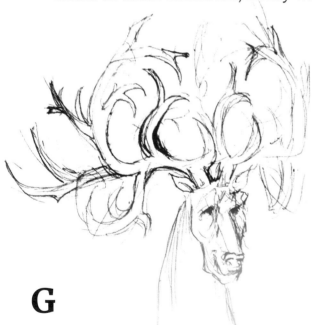

# G

**gales**—[DJD] a wind not tempestuous, yet stronger than a breeze. As the mighty poet Milton writes in *Paradise Regain'd*, "Winds / Of gentlest gale Arabian odors fann'd / From their soft wings, and Flora's earliest smells."

[WEB] 1. a strong current of air; a wind between a stiff breeze and a hurricane. The most violent gales are called tempests. 2. a moderate current of air; a breeze. "A little gale will soon disperse that cloud / And blow it to the source from whence it came: / The very beams will dry those vapours up, / For every cloud engenders not a storm" (Shakespeare's *3 Henry VI*). 3. a state of excitement, passion, or hilarity. 4. a song or story.

[M5] it seems to me that Dr. Johnson and Mr. Webster disagree. I suppose it is just a tempest in a teapot, or is that a breeze? At least Milton and Shakespeare agree, that a gale is closer to a gentle breeze than to a tempest. Or do they? "I'll deliver you all; / And promise you calm seas, auspicious gales, / And sail so expeditious that shall catch / Your royal fleet far off" (Shakespeare's *Tempest*).

**Gallant**—[WEB] 1. a man of mettle or spirit. 2. noble in bearing or spirit; brave; high-spirited; courageous; heroic; magnanimous; as a gallant youth; a gallant officer.

[M5] the Gallant rhymes with "pal" and "ant," and as Dr. Johnson stresses in his dictionary, you must stress the first syllable, the one that rhymes with "pal": GALLant.

**gasped**—[DJD] past tense of "gasp," which means: 1. to open the mouth wide to catch a breath. 2. to emit breath by opening the mouth convulsively. 3. to long for. This sense is, Dr. Johnson thinks, not proper, as nature never expresses desire by gasping.

**gay**—[WEB] 1. excited with merriment; manifesting sportiveness or delight; inspiring delight; merry. 2. brilliant in colors; splendid; fine; richly dressed. 3. loose; dissipated; lewd.

**gelatinous**—[WEB] of the nature or consistence of gelatin or jelly; resembling jelly; viscous.

**girth**—[WEB] 1. a band or strap which encircles the body; especially, one by which a saddle is fastened upon the back of a horse. 2. the measure round the body, as at the waist or belly; the circumference of anything. 3. a small horizontal brace or girder.

**gloats**—[DJD] to cast side glances as a timorous lover.

[WEB] to look steadfastly; to gaze.

[M5] the word may come from an old Icelandic word, "glotta," which means to smile scornfully. But its common meaning today, to look with intense satisfaction at having exceeded or beaten someone else, may well have come from the powerful and passionate English poet Lord Byron: "Nurtur'd in blood betimes, his heart delights / In vengeance gloating on another's pain." Poets can, over time, reshape, expand, or contract the sense and meanings of a word. Or they can remind you of a word's older or double meanings.

**gloom**—[DJD] 1. imperfect darkness; dismalness; obscurity; defect of light 2. cloudiness of aspect; heaviness of mind; sullenness. 3. to shine obscurely, as the twilight. This sense is not now in use.

**glorious**—[DJD] 1. boastful; proud; haughty; ostentatious. 2. noble; illustrious; excellent.

**glossary**—[DJD] a dictionary of obscure or antiquated words.

[M5] allow me to gloss, which means comment on, these words in the definition of "glossary": "obscure" means dark, difficult, not easily intelligible, abstruse; "antiquated" means old and out of fashion. This glossary explains a few old and hidden aspects of the liberal arts, so that they become less abstruse, which means hidden.

**gracious**—[DJD] 1. merciful; benevolent. 2. favorable; kind. 3. acceptable; favored. 4. virtuous; good. 5. excellent. 6. graceful; becoming.

**grasps**—[DJD] 1. to hold in the hand, to grip; to seize, to catch at; to struggle, to strive, to grapple. 2. the grip of the hand; possession, hold.

**grievesome**—[WEB] a variation of "grievous," which means causing grief or sorrow; painful; afflictive; hard to bear; offensive; harmful.

[M5] "-some," as suffix, to change a verb or noun into an adjective, can seem troublesome, but it can also be winsome, awesome, or, in the Nólle's case, woesome.

**grimy**—[WEB] 1. full of grime; begrimed; dirty; foul.

[M5] unrelated, technically, is another word that's too amusing not to share with you: "grimsir," which means a stern man. Don't be a grimsir.

**groom**—[WEB] to tend or care for, or to curry or clean, as a, horse.

# H

**Hai-chus**—[M5] "hai" means something like "yes" or "I agree" in Japanese, and "chu" is a word in Japanese for the sound of a kiss. Now, the use of words that describe things by sounding like the thing they describe, for instance, "boom," "crash," "gulp," "pop," "hum," and "gasp," is called onomatopœia. And according to the boldly named *Library of Universal Knowledge* (Volume 10, no less!), that fancy Greek word means the invention or making of names—name-making. Importantly, the "-pœia" part of that word is the ancient Greek source for our English words "poem," "poetry," and "poet." Poets often make new words and names. Would that make them onomatopœiaists?

**happenstantual**—[M5] unplanned, sudden, thoughtless.

**hardships**—[DJD] 1. injury; oppression. 2. inconvenience; fatigue.

**hath**—[M5] an old-fashioned and elevated way to say "has."

**haunting**—[M5] somehow familiar, yet unsettling, as whenever we creatures are in the presence of a spirit or ghost, or any presence which we cannot see.

**haywire**—[M5] if you've ever seen a bale of hay, bound with wire, then you know what this word means. And if you've ever seen a bale of hay's haywire break, coil out, and splay all over, you will understand the meaning of this very American farm phrase, "going haywire," which means to go a lot or a little bit crazy, as when the haywire breaks and goes wild. Americans understand the need for haywire and what goes wrong when the haywire breaks. We even sing about it in one of our favorite songs, "America the Beautiful": "Confirm thy soul in self-control, thy liberty in law." That, or go haywire!

**headsman**—[DJD] an executioner; one that cuts off heads.

**horde**—[WEB] a wandering troop or gang; especially, a clan or tribe of a nomadic people migrating from place to place for the sake of pasturage, plunder, etc.; a predatory multitude.

[M5] the word came slowly west from eastern languages, like the many, mighty nomadic tribes that invaded Europe during and after the fall of the Roman Empire.

**hubbub**—[DJD] 1. a tumult; a riot.

**humanitas**—[M5] the Roman philosopher, statesman, and playwright Seneca the Younger called *humanitas* "the idea of man" by which men mold themselves to completion, perfection, and happiness, as an artist sculpts a sculpture from the idea in his head. It is no small accomplishment to have in your head a good and accurate "idea of man." So let me give you a few entries from Dr. Johnson's Dictionary that begin to give us a sense of *humanitas*:

[DJD] 1. "humane" means kind, civil, benevolent, good-natured. 2. "humanity" means the nature of man, humankind, the collective body of mankind; benevolence, tenderness; philology; grammatical studies. 3. "humanize" means to soften, to make susceptible to tenderness and benevolence. The best example of this last word's use comes from the poet and diplomat Sir Henry Wotton, who, having lost his dear cousin and fellow diplomat, Sir Albertus Morton, wrote the following lines in a poem called "Tears Wept at the Grave of Sir Albertus Morton": "Here will I paint the characters of woe; / Here will I pay my tribute to the dead; / And here my faithful tears in showers shall flow, / To humanize the flints on which I tread." Wotton also wrote in a letter to a dear friend the following lines concerning his dearly departed cousin: "I received notice of Sir Albertus Morton, his departure from this world, who was dearer to me than mine own being in it: what a wound it is to my heart, you that knew him, and know me, will easily believe: but our Creator's will must be done, and unrepiningly received by his own creatures, who is the Lord of all nature and of all fortune, when he taketh to himself now one, then another, till that expected day, wherein it shall please him to dissolve the whole, and wrap up even the heaven itself as a scroll of parchment. This is the last philosophy that we must study upon earth; let us therefore, that yet remain here, as our days and friends waste, reinforce our love to each other; which of all virtues, both spiritual and moral, hath the highest privilege, because death itself cannot end it."

**humbug**—[WEB] 1. an imposition under fair pretenses; something contrived in order to deceive and mislead; a trick by cajolery; a hoax. 2. a spirit of deception; cajolery; trickishness. 3. one who deceives or misleads; a deceitful or trickish fellow; an imposter. Probably from "hum," meaning to impose, and "bug," meaning originally any frightening object, and now a frightening insect!

**humorous**—[WEB] 1. an obsolete meaning: moist; humid; watery. 2. subject to be governed by humor or caprice; irregular; capricious; whimsical. 3. full of humor, jocular; exciting laughter; playful; as, a humorous story or author; a humorous aspect or look. Note: The ancient physicians believed that there were four humors (the blood, phlegm, yellow bile or choler, and black bile or melancholy), on the relative proportion of which one's temperament and health depended.

[M5] the four humors are still used in poetry to help understand our moods and character. Not the real fluids, of course, but as a set of loose metaphors: too much blood, and you might be a sanguine, with quick passions that fade just as fast; too much phlegm makes a phlegmatic, who is always calm and maybe cold; too much choler, and you may be a leader, but meaner than you need to be; too much melancholy, then, sad to say, you may have something in common with the Nólle.

The ancient Greek doctor Hippocrates of Kos is said to have first developed the medical theory of humors as part of his medical arts, which, it is said, he would only teach to those who would swear a great and mighty oath to use medicine only ever to heal and never to do harm, nor give poison, nor teach these arts to any pupil unwilling to take the oath as well. The great majority of doctors in our history have sworn some version of this oath. If you are called to medicine, I don't recommend you use Hippocrates' humors to heal the *body*, but you might take a sacred oath "to do no harm," which may be good medicine for your heart.

**hypothetical**—[WEB] characterized by, or of the nature of, an hypothesis; conditional; assumed without proof, for the purpose of reasoning and deducing proof, or of accounting for some fact or phenomenon.

[M5] deductive reasoning involves making syllogisms. The most famous syllogism may be this: (1) All men are mortal; (2) Socrates is a man; (3) therefore, Socrates is mortal. A syllogism, in Logic, is a way of speaking or writing mental judgments that do not err. If (1) and (2) above are true, and they are, then (3) is necessarily true. For the conclusion to be true, the two hypotheticals have to be assumed as true.

The liberal art of Logic is part of the great Trivium, the three liberal arts of the human mind, namely Grammar, Logic, and Rhetoric. The liberal arts (in Latin *artes liberales*) are also called the arts of liberty, the arts required for being a free and happy human being. There are other arts of liberty, like law, music, and geometry. Without these arts, it is so much harder to be free.

**I**

**illustrated**—[DJD] past tense of "illustrate," meaning to brighten with light; to brighten with honor; to explain, to clear, to elucidate.

[WEB] to adorn with pictures, as a book or subject; to elucidate with pictures. That beloved, old, and too often mocked schoolmaster Holofernes used the word: "this most gallant, illustrate, and learned gentleman, before the princess, I say none so fit to present the Nine Worthies" (*Love's Labour's Lost*).

[M5] the Nine Worthies are examples of three sets of three heroes, from Greco-Roman pagan, Jewish Old Testament, and Christian medieval times. I suspect Shakespeare disagreed with the traditional choice of the pagan worthies of Hector of Troy, Julius Caesar, and Alexander the Great because, for instance, in one of his plays he repeatedly calls Alexander the Great as Alexander the Big, but the poor fellow who speaks the line has an accent, and so it becomes "Alexander the Pig"! In any case, they are all nine designed to illustrate various heroic virtues of leadership, which is a most challenging task for any teacher.

**imagine**—[M5] a disciplined imagination is one of those special powers of humans that set us apart from the other mammals, for even though sleeping dogs can dream of chasing rabbits, those same faithful beasts cannot make themselves dream of chasing rabbits when they are awake. Try it: "Blue Whale." Think of that largest of all mammals in your head. Amazing! The biggest thing in the sea is now swimming in your little head's mysterious ocean of memory! Control of your imagination is one way of separating yourself from the beasts!

**immersed**—[DJD] 1. to put under water. 2. to sink or cover deep. 3. to keep in a state of intellectual depression. As the cleric, politician, and writer Francis Atterbury wrote, "We are prone to engage ourselves with the business, the pleasures, and the amusements of the this world; we give ourselves up too greedily to the pursuit, and immerse ourselves too deeply in the enjoyment of them."

**Indiana**—[M5] the nineteenth state to enter the union of the United States of America, this beautiful land of new-mown hay and moonlit rivers was once, many thousands of years ago, half-covered in a mile-high glacier, during the great ice-age.

**indignant**—[DJD] 1. angry, raging, inflamed at once with anger and disdain. The mighty poet Milton once compared the Persian tyrant Xerxes to the devils in hell: "So, if great things to small may be compared, / Xerxes, the liberty of Greece to yoke / . . . / Came to the sea, and, over Hellespont / Bridging his way, Europe with Asia joined; / And scourged with many a stroke the indignant waves."

[M5] Milton knew the ancient doings of Xerxes because this story has been passed down for many generations in the *Histories* of the ancient Greek Herodotus. In that work, Herodotus tells of Xerxes's great pride and his desire to dominate the neighboring peoples, the Greeks of Hellas. Persia and Hellas were and are separated by a mighty channel of water, the Hellespont. Xerxes built great bridges for his army to cross over and crush the Greeks. Here is how Herodotus described Xerxes' rage on those shores:

"When, therefore, the channel had been bridged successfully, it happened that a great storm arising broke the whole work to pieces, and destroyed all that had been done. So when Xerxes heard of it he was full of wrath, and straightway gave orders that the Hellespont should receive three hundred lashes, and that a pair of fetters should be cast into it. Nay, I have even heard it said that he bade the branders take their irons and therewith brand the Hellespont. It is certain that he commanded those who scourged the waters to utter, as they lashed them, these barbarian and wicked words: 'Thou bitter water, thy lord lays on thee this punishment because thou hast wronged him without a cause, having suffered no evil at his hands. Verily King Xerxes will cross thee, whether thou wilt or no. Well dost thou deserve that no man should honor thee with sacrifice; for thou art of a truth a treacherous and unsavory river.' While the sea was thus punished by his orders, he likewise commanded that the overseers of the work should lose their heads."

Thank God, this tyrant was roundly defeated by the far fewer forces of the brave and clever Greeks.

**Inowallah**—[M5] "Inowallah" begins with a short "i" sound as in "in." Then add no-WAH-lah. So IN-no-WAH-lah—Inowallah. The singular and plural of the Inowallah is strangely tricky: "Inowallah" or "Inowallahs" are both the plural, and "Inowall" is the singular. The word becomes a plural when one adds a breath ("-ah") or two ("-ahs").

**insane**—[DJD] mad; from the Latin for broken or unhealthy: *in-* meaning not and *-sanus* meaning whole or healthy; not healthy or not whole, especially with respect to an unhealthy or broken mind.

[M5] when people act insanely, we often say that they have "lost their senses"; how important, then, must the five senses be for keeping the mind healthy. For a mind without the five senses is like a home with no windows or doors to the outside. How unhealthy such a stuffy cave would be!

**invigorates**—[DJD] to endue with vigor; to strengthen; to animate; to enforce.

**ironically**—[DJD] by the use of irony, which means a mode of speech in which the meaning is contrary to the words. As the gift-bearing Francis Bacon said of the Greek philosopher, "Socrates was pronounced by the oracle of Delphos to be the wisest man of Greece, which he would turn from himself ironically, saying, there could be nothing in him to verify the oracle, except this, that he was not wise, and knew it; and others were not wise, and knew it not."

[M5] irony comes from an ancient Greek word basically meaning "other speak" or "speaking in an otherly way," and irony can mean to speak of something in some other way than directly to the purpose. As George Puttenham put it in his famous *Arte of English Poesie*, irony is "the dry mock." If you can detect irony, you can see many truths hidden in falsehoods and even falsehoods hidden in truths. Ironically, much that lies beneath the surface tells us something more, if we've the wit to see it. As the statesman-poet Thomas More surely said and as Shakespeare could never, ever possibly have written, "Wit, judge not things by the outward show, / The eye oft mistakes, right well you do know."

# J

**jagged**—[WEB] having jags; having rough, sharp notches, protuberances, or teeth; cleft; divided; as, jagged rocks.

[M5] "jagged" can be pronounced as one syllable, as in "zagged" in "zig-zagged," or it can be pronounced with two syllables as in the "The Tale of the Tanglis." But how do you know which pronunciation? From the rhythm of the poem. Try reading the poem both ways, and see how the two syllables of "JAG-ged" sound more musical. Try the same for "aged" in the first line of "The Gallant and the Golden Birch." The more you can feel meter, the more you can pronounce new words in poetry. And you will soon become more learned too. (Did you just say "LEARN-ed" like I taught you to?)

**Jargontalky**—[M5] distant cousin to the Jabberwocky; pronounced JAR-gon-TALK-y.

**John**—[M5] the first name of my friend and illustrator, Mr. Folley; the name is more than 2,000 years old, and it originally meant "favored by God" in the ancient Hebrew language. If the word is not capitalized, the meaning is changed.

**jolly**—[DJD] 1. gay, merry, airy, cheerful, lively, jovial.

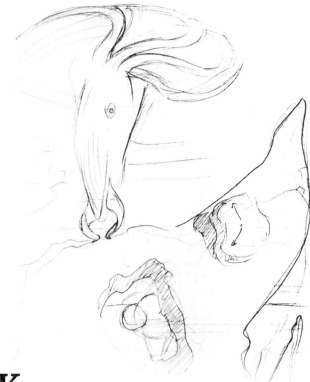

# K

**Kalondahres**—[M5] "Kal-" as in California; "-on-" as "lawn"; "-dahr-" as in "dar-ling"; "-es" as in the Oakland "A's." So CAL-lawn-DAR-A's or KALonDAHRes—so Kalondahres. Pronounce it one way always.

**keen**—[WEB] 1. sharp; having a fine edge or point; as, a keen razor, or a razor with a keen edge. "A bow he bare and arrows bright and keen" (Chaucer's Prologue to the *Canterbury Tales*). 2. acute of mind; sharp; penetrating; having or expressing mental acuteness; as, a man of keen understanding; a keen look; keen features. "Counsel may stop awhile what will not stay; / For when we rage, advice is often seen / By blunting us to make our wits more keen" (Shakespeare's "A Lover's Complaint").

**kidney bean**—[WEB] a sort of bean, so named from its shape. It is of the genus *Phaseolus* (*Phaseolus vulgaris*).

[M5] thank God for words of common use, like kidney bean for *Phaseolus vulgaris*.

**kindled**—[DJD] the past tense of "kindle," which means: 1. to set on fire; to light; to make burn. 2. to inflame the passions; to exasperate; to animate; to heat; to fire the mind. 3. to catch fire. 4. from the Old English or Saxon *cennan*, to bring forth: a mammal giving birth. As Rosiland says to Orlando when he asks her, "O: Are you native of this place? / R: As the coney that you see dwells where she is kindled" (Shakespeare's *As You Like It*).

[M5] a coney or cony is a rabbit, a mammal famous for its prodigious kindling or *cennan*, in Old English. Because Old English is very old and Middle English is less so, I like to say that now we all speak Young English!

**kinship**—[WEB] family relationship.

# L

**lacking**—[WEB] 1. blaming; finding fault with. 2. being without or destitute of; wanting; needing.

**laden**—[WEB] loaded; freighted; burdened; as, a laden vessel; a laden heart. "Woe to the sinful nation, a people laden with iniquity, a wicked seed, ungracious children: they have forsaken the Lord, they have blasphemed the Holy One of Israel, they are gone away backwards" (Is 1:4).

[M5] or as the rash Mark Antony utters in fitful despair at his great shame: "Hark! the land bids me tread

no more upon't; / It is ashamed to bear me! Friends, come hither: / I am so lated in the world, that I / Have lost my way for ever: I have a ship / Laden with gold; take that, divide it; fly, / And make your peace with Caesar" (Shakespeare's *Antony and Cleopatra*).

**lame**—[DJD] 1. crippled; disabled in the limbs. 2. hobbling; not smooth; alluding to the feet of a verse. As Dryden's satire holds, in the voice of a stoic philosopher Persius, who makes fun of the Roman tyrant-emperor Nero's horrible poetry and the verses of all those who slavishly imitate the fearsome, artless, yet powerful bullies of any culture: "Our authors write, / Whether in prose, or verse, 'tis all the same; / The prose is fustian, and the numbers lame." 3. imperfect; unsatisfactory.

**lapping**—[WEB] from the verb "to lap," which means: 1. to be turned or folded; to lie partly upon or by the side of something, or of one another; as, the cloth laps back; the boats lap; the edges lap. 2. to take up drink or food with the tongue; to drink or feed by licking up something; or to make a sound like that produced by taking up drink with the tongue. As Sir Bedivere twice lied to the dying King Arthur, "I heard the ripple washing in the reeds, / And the wild water lapping on the crag" (Alfred, Lord Tennyson's "Morte d'Arthur").

**lard**—[DJD] 1. the grease of swine. 2. bacon; the flesh of swine. 3. to stuff with bacon; to fatten; to mix with something else by way of improvement.

**Las Vaquitas**—[M5] "Las" means the in Spanish. See also the "Vaquitas" entry below.

**Latin**—[DJD] an exercise practiced by schoolchildren, who turn English into Latin, which means anything written or spoken in the language of the old Romans.

[M5] Latin is one of the two great classical languages along with ancient Greek. It is a language of law, culture, philosophy, history, religion, and piety. If you learn Latin, you will have a key to whole worlds of goodness, truth, and beauty, for so many of the very best things have been spoken and written in the Latin language.

**lay**—[DJD] 1. a song or poem. From the French, it is said originally to signify sorrow or complaint, and then to have been transferred to poems written to express sorrow. The French is derived from the Latin *lessus*, meaning a funeral song or lamentation. 2. grassy ground; meadow; ground unplowed, and kept for cattle.

**liberty**—[M5] 1. the freedom to choose the good; a state of one's will that permits virtuous choices; the absence of sin (what the Roman Seneca the Younger called *peccatus*). 2. the political or social state, under rule of law, most in accord with happiness and virtue; in Cicero's *On the Orator*, he argues that a republic should foster *salus ac libertas*, or prosperity and liberty. 3. ability to move the body, free of physical limitations or chains. Liberty is so very important and such a deeply good thing.

**liken**—[DJD] 1. to represent as having resemblance; to compare.

**liméd**—[DJD] to have been smeared with lime, a viscous substance drawn over twigs, which catches and entangles the wings of birds that light upon it. As the manifold and clever Proteus advises, "You must lay lime, to tangle her desires, / By wailful sonnets, whose composed rhymes / Should be full fraught with serviceable vows" (Shakespeare's *Two Gentlemen of Verona*).
   [M5] please speak this word as I pronounce it to you, with two syllables: LIE-med or LIME-ed—liméd.

**listen**—[M5] the most mysterious of the five senses, hearing or listening involves not just sounds but also, Augustine tells us in his *Confessions*, words and song that enter "the ear of the heart." What songs we listen to, what words we take in, don't just enter the ear of the head, but also the ear of the heart. Our hearts are helped by healthy songs and harmed by harmful ones. And if a harmful song ever enters our ears, hopefully we can helpfully heal our hearts if afterwards we're careful to let good songs and good words enter that inner sanctum of our souls, through "the ear of the heart."

**loamy**—[WEB] 1. consisting of loam; partaking of the nature of loam; resembling loam, which is a mixture of sand, clay, and other materials, used for making molds for large castings, often without a pattern. Loam may also mean a kind of soil; an earthy mixture of clay and sand, with organic matter to which its fertility is chiefly due.

**locals**—[M5] people of a particular place, spot, location, region, often with their own particular customs and affections.

**loch**—[DJD] Scottish for a lake.
   [M5] the word is pronounced like "lock."

**locks**—[DJD] 1. a quantity of hair or wool hanging together. "His grizly locks, long growen and unbound, / Disordered hung about his shoulders round" (Spenser's *Faerie Queene*). 2. any enclosure. 3. an instrument composed of springs and bolts, used to fasten doors or chests. 4. a hug or grapple.

**loom**—[WEB] 1. to appear above the surface either of sea or land, or to appear enlarged, or distorted and indistinct, as a distant object, a ship at sea, or a mountain, esp. from atmospheric influences; as, the ship looms large; the land looms high. 2. a frame or machine, in which a weaver forms cloth out of thread; a machine for interweaving yarn or threads into a fabric, as in knitting or lace making.

[M5] as Melville wrote in *Moby Dick*, "Ah, mortal! then, be heedful; for so, in all this din of the great world's loom, thy subtlest thinkings may be overheard afar."

**Louisiana**—[M5] the eighteenth state to enter the union of the United States of America, this hazy land of sunshine, bayous, and pelicans (the most self-sacrificing birds in America) was formed in part by the great glacial melt to its north during the thaw of the ice age, which carried silt and mud down the mighty Mississippi River to create the great coastal marshes, Mississippi Delta, and the land that is now Plaquemines Parish. Looking at maps of Louisiana will amaze you!

**love**—[M5] love is a great mystery and yet everyone knows what it means. There are good loves and bad loves. But in the First Epistle of John, we read, "He that loveth not, knoweth not God, for God is love." The Latin here is "*Deus caritas est*"; "God charity is" or "God is love." This Roman word for love (*caritas*) is very special. Dear old Marcus Tullius Cicero—his friends still call him Tully!—thought so: "For this is, without a doubt, the life of a tyrant, in which no good faith, no love [*caritas*], and no long-standing good will can prosper and in which every thing causes suspicion and worry—in such a life there is no place for friendship." Tully also thought virtue (*virtus*) and love or charity (*caritas*) were more or less the same thing.

**lugged**—[WEB] the past tense of "lug," which means: 1. to move slowly and heavily. 2. to pull with force; to haul; to drag along; to carry with difficulty, as something heavy or cumbersome. 3. move about, along, heavily and slowly; to drag.

**luminous**—[DJD] shining, emitting light; enlightened; bright.

**Lundregun**—[M5] this hungry mammal—if it is a mammal—sounds like "Tundra" and "gun," but with an L and run together: LUNDregun.

**lymph**—[WEB] 1. a spring of water; hence, water, or a pure, transparent liquid like water. 2. a fibrinous material exuded from the blood vessels in inflammation. In the process of healing it is either absorbed, or is converted into connective tissue binding the inflamed surfaces together.

# M

**magicked**—[DJD] from "magick," which possesses several, very different meanings: 1. the secret operations of natural powers. 2. the art of putting in action the power of spirits: it was supposed that both good and bad spirits were subject to magick; yet magick was in general held unlawful; sorcery; enchantment. 3. acting or doing by powers superior to the known power of nature. 4. necromantick; incantating. As the devilish leader of the foul witches in Shakespeare's *Macbeth* sings, "Upon the corner of the moon / There hangs a vaporous drop profound; I'll catch it ere it come to ground: / And that distill'd by magic sleights / Shall raise such artificial sprites / As by the strength of their illusion / Shall draw him on to his confusion."

**mamás**—[M5] a somewhat fancy, British way to pronounce "mamas," with the stress on the second syllable: maMAS instead of the American MAmas. Our

English language, among other precious things, comes in large part from the British Isles.

mammals—[M5] it was very likely the surgeon, classicist, poet, and naturalist Dr. John M. Good who first coined the word "mammal." Here is a passage from his *Book of Nature*, simply put: "We ascend now to the FIRST and HIGHEST CLASS—to the rank of animals which is most complicated in form and most competent in power. This class is chiefly distinguished by the possession of lungs, and an organ for suckling; and most of its kinds possess four supporters in the shape of hands or feet, or both. To this last character the class was formerly called by its classic name, QUADRUPED, Latin for FOUR-FOOTED. As some kinds under it, however, are possessed of no supporters of any sort, either hands or feet (like the Tanglis!); others have four hands and no feet (sort of like the Evol!); and others, again, have two of each (like the Dally!), the absurdity of keeping such a name must be obvious to everyone; and hence it has been correctly and elegantly exchanged, by Linnaeus, for that of the class MAMMALIA, from the mammary or suckling organ which belongs to every kind of the class, as it stands at present, and to no kind of animal outside that class; and which, as we have no fair synonym for it in our own tongue, I shall beg leave now, as I have on various other occasions, to call MAMMALS."

A mammal himself, who suckled milk from his mother when he was a baby, Dr. John M. Good was also named by his father after his uncle John, who wrote an essay called "Self-Knowledge," in which he gives the following advice more or less: "In our morning self-examination, it will be proper to remember that we cannot preserve throughout the day that calm and even temper we may then be in; that we shall very probably meet with some things to ruffle us, some attack on our weak side. Place a guard there now. Or, however, if no incidents happen to discompose us, our tempers will vary; our thoughts will flow pretty much with our blood; and the dispositions of the mind be a good deal governed by the motions of the animal spirits; our souls will be serene or cloudy, our tempers volatile or phlegmatic, and our inclinations sober or irregular, according to the briskness or sluggishness of the circulation of the animal fluids, whatever may be the cause or immediate occasion of that. . . . Pious thoughts and purposes in the morning will set a guard upon the soul, and fortify it under all the temptations of the day." What a wise family of mammals the Goods are!

mantle—[WEB] 1. a loose garment to be worn over other garments; an enveloping robe; a cloak. Hence, figuratively, a covering or concealing envelope.

mar—[DJD] to injure; to spoil; to hurt; to mischief; to damage.

masses—[DJD] 1. a body; a lump; a continuous quantity; a large quantity; bulk; vast body. 2. congeries; assemblage indistinct. 3. gross body; the general. "The mass of the people have opened their eyes, and will not be governed by Clodius and Curio at the head of their myrmidons" (Jonathan Swift's *A Discourse on the Contests and Dissensions between the Nobles and the Commons in Athens and Rome*). 4. the service of the Roman church.

Matthew—[M5] a famous name of one of the twelve apostles and four evangelists, who wrote the first of the four gospels in the New Testament of the Holy Bible or Sacred Scriptures. Each of the evangelists are represented by an animal: John by an eagle; Luke by a bull with wings;

Mark by a lion with wings; and Matthew, curiously, by what looks like an angel, but is really a man with wings, because his gospel is most concerned with the humanity of Jesus Christ. The name in ancient Hebrew means "gift of God," which our humanity surely is. See the entry for "humanitas."

**Mehan**—[M5] my last name; the "h" is silent, so it sounds like the first two syllables in the phrase "me 'n you." The stress is on the first syllable, so you say ME(h)an.

**mildly**—[DJD] tenderly; not severely; gently; not violently.

[WEB] in a mild manner, "mild" meaning: gentle; pleasant; kind; soft; bland; clement; hence, moderate in degree or quality; the opposite of harsh, severe, irritating, violent, disagreeable, etc.; applied to persons and things; as, a mild disposition; a mild eye; a mild air; a mild medicine.

**minding**—[WEB] from the verb "to mind," meaning: 1. to fix the mind or thoughts on; to regard with attention; to treat as of consequence; to consider; to heed; to mark; to note. "Being of one mind one towards another. Not minding high things, but consenting to the humble. Be not wise in your own conceits" (Rom 12:16). Or "My lord, you nod: you do not mind the play" (Shakespeare's *Taming of the Shrew*). 2. to occupy one's self with; to employ one's self about; to attend to; as, to mind one's business. 3. to obey; as, to mind parents; the dog minds his master. 4. to have in mind; to purpose. 5. to put in mind; to remind. 6. to give attention or heed; to obey.

[M5] the ancient Roman's spoke of a virtue, presence of mind, in Latin called *praesentia animi*. Every virtue has an opposing vice, and the vice opposing presence of mind is distraction. Having the virtue of presence of mind in full is the achievement of a lifetime of struggle against distraction. In a funny little way, memorizing poems like those in this book can strengthen the memory and aid your presence of mind!

**mint leaves**—[M5] the Gallant minds the mint leaves, which grow below the northern trees, because he does not want to crush them. The Gallant knows the children want to pick those mint leaves, chew them, and taste their minty flavors! Good and grand old mammals tend to remember the wishes of others and especially the wishes of little ones.

**miserly**—[DJD] like a miser; very covetous; sordid.

[M5] greedily; *miser* in Latin means wretched, sad, pitiable. Just so is the poor fellow who never learns to be generous or who fails to see the generosity he has been shown. The miser tends to horde both money and his thanks, the one never leaves his sight and the other never leaves his lips!

**mist**—[DJD] 1. a low thin cloud; a small thin rain not perceived in single drops. As the loyal poet Sir John Denham wrote of the role of Chaucer's poetry in social life, "Old Chaucer, like the morning star, / His light those mists and clouds dissolv'd / Which our dark nation long involv'd" ("Mr. Abraham Cowley's Death, and Burial amongst the Ancient Poets"). 2. anything that dims or darkens.

**Mixxy**—[M5] barely sounds like "tricksy" but mixed with an "M."

**mole**—[M5] this little mammal is blind, like the ancient Greek poet Homer, who had to rely—like the mole—on his other senses and—unlike the mole—on his mind's eye.

**money**—[M5] a thing that humans alternately love or hate with too much passion whenever they mistake its value.

**monsters**—[WEB] 1. something of unnatural size, shape, or quality; a prodigy; an enormity; a marvel. 2. specifically, an animal or plant departing greatly from the usual type.

3. any thing or person of unnatural or excessive ugliness, deformity, wickedness, or cruelty.

**Montana**—[M5] the forty-first state to enter the union of the United States of America, this land of gold and silver, meadowlarks and bitterroot, is still home to some of the ancient glaciers that once covered so much of North America. Like giants of old, the glaciers still lurk high in the mountains of the great Continental Divide.

**morbid**—[DJD] diseased; in a state contrary to health.

**morn**—[DJD] the first part of the day; the morning. "Morn" is not used but by poets.

**Muses**—[M5] nine goddess sisters of Greek mythology; the poet Hesiod, in his *Theogony*, sings of them upon their hallowed Mount Helicon, where they sing in shady glades of dusk and dawn, those famed daughters of Zeus and Memory. Each has a name, and each is said to have discovered some number of the arts. For instance, Terpsichore discovered dance; Polymnia discovered divine hymnody, geometry, and grammar; Ourania discovered astronomy; and Calliope, greatest of all the Muses, aids all poets who wish to sing of heroes and myth and to help all society, all its leaders and citizens, by means of the crowning liberal art, rhetoric, the peaceful art of persuasion through speech, and song. The great poet Virgil, in his *Aeneid*, asked for the Muse to inspire him, to help him remember the causes of his song. And Shakespeare wished for a Muse of Fire to help him sing the history of kings. God, mixed with memory, artfully mixed with a poet's song? Little wonder, then—or perhaps what a wonder!—that poets have always sought a Muse to light the fires of their imagination! But be careful, for every fire burns.

**myth**—[WEB] 1. a story of great but unknown age which originally embodied a belief regarding some fact or phenomenon of experience, and in which often the forces of nature and of the soul are personified; an ancient legend of a god, a hero, the origin of a race, etc.; a wonder story of prehistoric origin; a popular fable which is, or has been, received as historical. 2. a person or thing existing only in imagination, or whose actual existence is not verifiable.

[M5] one might say that a good Myth is a true and loving Mind wrapped in word, image, and song.

**mythic**—[M5] see entry for "mythical" just below.

**mythical**—[DJD] from "mystical," which means: 1. sacredly obscure. 2. involving some secret meaning; emblematical. 3. obscure; secret.

# N

**natural**—[WEB] 1. fixed or determined by nature; pertaining to the constitution of a thing; belonging to native character;

according to nature; essential; characteristic; not artificial, foreign, assumed, put on, or acquired; as, the natural growth of animals or plants; the natural motion of a gravitating body; natural strength or disposition; the natural heat of the body; natural color. 2. conformed to the order, laws, or actual facts of nature; consonant to the methods of nature; according to the stated course of things, or in accordance with the laws which govern events, feelings, etc.; not exceptional or violent; legitimate; normal; regular; as, the natural consequence of crime; a natural death. 3. having to do with the existing system of things; dealing with, or derived from, the creation, or the world of matter and mind, as known by man; within the scope of human reason or experience; not supernatural; as, a natural law; natural science; history. 4. conformed to truth or reality; as: (a) springing from true sentiment; not artificial or exaggerated; said of action, delivery, etc.; as, a natural gesture, tone, etc.; (b) resembling the object imitated; true to nature; according to the life; said of anything copied or imitated; as, a portrait is natural. 5. having the character or sentiments properly belonging to one's position; not unnatural in feelings. 6. connected by the ties of consanguinity. "He had natural friends, with nearer claims on his charity" (J. H. Newman *A Tale of the Third Century*).

[DJD] 1. tender; affectionate by nature. 2. unaffected; according to reality. 3. opposed to violent; as, a natural death.

[M5] Cicero's *On Duties*, in Latin called *De Officiis*, one of the greatest books of all time, has much to teach about this word. *On Duties* was the very next book off the printing press after Gutenberg's Bible, and it was the second-most copied manuscript of the medieval monks, after the Sacred Scriptures, for a thousand years. That book was once (and can be again) second nature to us. See the entry for "nature" just below.

**nature**—[WEB] 1. the existing system of things; the world of matter and mind; the whole of creation; the universe. 2. the personified sum and order of causes and effects; powers producing existing phenomena. 3. conformity to that which is natural, as distinguished from that which is artificial, or forced, or remote from actual experience. 4. physical constitution or existence; vital powers; the natural life. "Oppressed nature sleeps" (Shakespeare's *King Lear*). 5. natural affection or reverence.

**nay**—[DJD] 1. no; an adverb of negation. 2. not only so, but more. 3. a word of refusal. The intriguing journalist Sir Roger L'Estrange put it in his retelling of Aesop's fables: "The fox made several excuses, but the stork would not be said nay; so that at last he promised him to come."

**neither**—[DJD] not either; a negative particle.

**nettle**—[DJD] a stinging herb well known. "The strawberry grows beneath the nettle" (Shakespeare's *Henry V*).

**nightingale**—[DJD] from the Old English "galan," meaning to sing, with "night." A small bird that sings in the night with remarkable melody; Philomel.

[M5] the friendly poet Chaucer begins his *Canterbury Tales* describing small birds making melody, put to it by nature in their hearts, which he called their "courages." It is a joy to be able to recite the first eighteen lines of the beautiful Prologue of the *Canterbury Tales* in the original Middle English, although it takes hard work and stout "courages" to memorize it well. (For instance, "night" is pronounced "nikt" in Middle English, as in a singing niktingale.) Students have had to memorize those first lines for centuries, thanking their parents, their teachers . . . eventually!

**night-shirt**—[WEB] a kind of nightgown for men.

**nimble**—[WEB] light and quick in motion; moving with ease and celerity; lively; swift.

**Nólle**—[M5] this mammal's name rhymes with "Vólle" and "okay," but stress it like NOL-le, okay? And I have a confession to make: the Vólle and Nólle rhyme because they are both meant to fly further up and away, deeper into the heavens, and not wallow in a cave or a pool, like some graceless Hippo.

**noblest**—[WEB] possessing eminence, elevation, dignity, etc.; above whatever is low, mean, degrading, or dishonorable; magnanimous; as, a noble nature or action; a noble heart. From the Latin *noscere*, meaning to know.

    [M5] Cicero used the Latin word *honestum*, which we translate as virtue or the noble or the honorable.

**nonetheless**—[M5] a funny way of saying, "Despite what I've said, there's something more."

**nor**—[WEB] a negative particle, of speech. "But lay up to yourselves treasures in heaven: where neither the rust nor moth doth consume, and where thieves do not break through, nor steal" (Mt 6:20).

**numinous**—[M5] anything associated with the dual meaning of the Latin word *numen* which concerns both the divine will and spiritual power, as well as the nodding of one's head.

# O

**O**—[WEB] an exclamation used in calling or directly addressing a person or personified object; also, as an emotional or impassioned exclamation expressing pain, grief, surprise, desire, fear, etc.

**oafish**—[DJD] stupid; dull; doltish.

**obscurity**—[DJD] 1. darkness; want of light. 2. unnoticed state; privacy. "You are not meant for obscurity designed, / But, like the sun, must cheer all human kind" (Dryden's *Tyrannic Love or, the Royal Martyr*).

**Oominoos**—[M5] we say it OO-min-oos, and it almost rhymes with "tomb in use."

113

Plet
in
foreground on

# P

**panel**—[DJD] 1. a square, or piece of any matter inserted between other bodies. 2. a schedule or roll, containing the names of such jurors, as the sheriff provides to pass upon a trial. And empaneling a jury is nothing but the entering them into the sheriff's roll or book.

[M5] in colleges and universities, panels involve gathering a group of speakers together or, more rarely, a group of thinkers, or—rarest of all!—a group of thinkers who can also speak.

**papás**—[M5] a somewhat fancy, British way to pronounce "papas," with the stress on the second syllable: paPAS instead of the American PApas.

**Patagónia**—[M5] part of South America named after a mythical race of giants called the Patagón. It's a big place, with big people, and big mythical mammals too!

**peace**—[DJD] 1. rest from any commotion, stillness from riots and tumults, quiet from suits and disturbances. 2. rest, quiet, content; freedom from terror; heavenly rest. "Well, peace be with him

that made us heavy! / Peace be with us, lest we be heavier!" (Shakespeare's 2 *Henry IV*). 3. reconciliation of differences. 4. respite from war.

[M5] the great Roman humanists, and later Christian Humanists, all cared deeply for peace, and they knew that the liberal art of rhetoric does much to secure peace. As Cicero writes in his *De Oratore* or *On the Orator*, "Among every free people, and most especially in peaceful and tranquil societies, the art of oratory has always flowered foremost and ever ruled the rest." Peace requires having the right words put in the right way at the right time. Blessed be gentle peace.

**peal**—[DJD] 1. a succession of loud sounds: as, of bells, thunder, canon, loud instruments. 2. it is once used by Shakespeare for a low dull noise, but improperly.

**pelting**—[DJD] striking with something thrown. "Poor naked wretches wheresoe'er you are / That bide the pelting of this pitiless storm!" (Shakespeare's *King Lear*).

[M5] if something is pelting you like a rainstorm, it may be, as Shakespeare put it elsewhere, a "sling or arrow of outrageous fortune," but it may more likely be a drop of "the gentle rain from heaven."

**perch**—[DJD] 1. a very nutritive fish. 2. a measure of five yards and half; a pole. 3. something on which birds can roost or sit.

**perhaps**—[WEB] by chance; peradventure; perchance; it may be.

**periegetic**—[M5] a periegetic song is a travel song, a song about a journey, like Odysseus' tale of his journeys, as sung by Homer, or like Aeneas' recounting of his wanderings to Queen Dido, in Virgil's *Aeneid*, or like the song sung by the souls in Dante's *Purgatorio* as they were ferried to Mt. Purgatory: "*In exitu Israel de Aegypto!*" / They chanted all together in one voice, With whatso in that psalm is after written" (2.46–48).

**per se**—[M5] a troublesome Latin phrase that the Evol really ought not to have foisted on the poor Dally, who hasn't studied Latin yet. The Latin literally means through itself, by itself; used for considering a thing as itself, in itself.

**pitiable**—[DJD] deserving pity.

**pity**—[DJD] compassion; sympathy with misery; tenderness for pain or uneasiness. "An ant dropt into the water; a woodpigeon took pity of her, and threw her a little bough" (L'Estrange's *Fables*).

**Plee**—[M5] this mammal is very hard to see, but very easy to hear! Like many things that are real, the Plee is known through the ears, not the eyes, nose, tongue, or hand.

**plead**—[WEB] 1. to argue in support of a claim, or in defense against the claim of another; to urge reasons for or against a thing; to attempt to persuade one by argument or supplication; to speak by way of persuasion; as, to plead for the life of a criminal; to plead with a judge or with a father. 2. in law, to present an answer, by allegation of fact; to make an allegation of fact in a cause; to carry on the allegations of the respective parties in a cause; to carry on a suit or plea.

**pleased**—[WEB] experiencing pleasure.

**plods**—[DJD] 1. to toil; to moil; to drudge; to travel. 2. to travel laboriously. 3. to study closely and dully. "Universal plodding prisons up / The nimble spirits in the arteries; / As motion and long-during action tires / The sinewy vigor of the traveler" (Shakespeare's *Love's Labour's Lost*).

**plumes**—[DJD] 1. feather of birds. 2. feather worn as an ornament. 3. pride;

towering mien. 4. token of honor; prize of contest.

**prance**—[DJD] 1. to spring and bound in high mettle. As the witty-wise John Gay wrote, "With mud filled high, the rumbling carts draw near, / Now rule the prancing steeds, laced charioteer." 2. to ride gallantly and ostentatiously. 3. to move in a warlike or showy manner.

**prate**—[DJD] to talk carelessly and without weight; to chatter; to tattle; to be loquacious; to prattle.

[M5] while on pilgrimage with the Host of an inn, the dear poet Chaucer sang a song called the "Tale of Sir Thopas," which his Host hated very much: "By God, said he, for plainly, at a word, / Your crusty rhyming is not worth a turd! / You do not a thing but spend the time. / Sir, at a word, thou shalt no longer rhyme." Poets tend to prate.

**preens**—[DJD] to trim the feathers of birds, to enable them to glide more easily through the air.

[M5] preening is for the birds.

**presume**—[DJD] 1. to suppose; to believe without previous examination; to affirm without immediate proof.

**prick**—[DJD] 1. to pierce with a small puncture. 2. to form or erect with an acuminated point.

[M5] "acuminated" is a fancy way to say "ending in a point."

**pride**—[DJD] 1. inordinate and unreasonable self-esteem. "I can feel his pride / peep through each part of him" (Shakespeare's *Henry VIII*). 2. insolence; rude treatment of others; insolent exultation. 3. dignity of manner; loftiness of air. 4. generous elation of heart. "The honest pride of conscious virtue" (Edmund Smith's *Phedra and Hippolitus*). 5. elevation; dignity. "A falcon, towering in her pride of place, / Was by a mousing owl hawkt at and killed" (Shakespeare's *Macbeth*). 6. ornament, show, decoration; splendor, ostentation.

[WEB] 1. loftiness; prime; glory. 2. a small European lamprey.

[M5] also, what we call a fearsome family of lions.

**primate**—[WEB] one of the highest order of mammals. It includes man, together with the apes and monkeys.

[DJD] the chief ecclesiastick, which means the chief person dedicated to the ministries of religion.

**print**—[M5] print is a lesser form of writing than cursive, in the same way a print of a painting is a lesser form of art than a painting. To think beautiful thoughts, it is always best to write them beautifully too.

**promise**—[DJD] 1. declaration of some benefit to be conferred. 2. performance of a promise; grant of the thing promised. 3. hopes; expectations.

[M5] in his *On Duties*, Cicero speaks of a great and noble ancient Roman, Regulus, who set an example for all the world by keeping his promise to the wicked Carthaginians, even though it cost him his very life. Rome, Cicero taught, was strong because everyone trusted their word, because they kept their promises.

**proper**—[DJD] 1. peculiar; not belonging to more; not common. 2. noting an individual. 3. one's own, as when the Duke of Venice falsely and rashly promises, "The bloody book of law / You shall yourself read in the bitter letter, / After your own sense; yes, though our proper son / Stood in your action" (Shakespeare's *Othello*). 4. natural; original. 5. fit; accommodated; adapted; suitable; qualified.

[M5] the proper, or finding what belongs to what, is a much greater matter than these definitions let on. Cicero and the Romans developed this idea of the proper (in Latin *proprium*), and it is in our day one of the rarest kinds of knowledge. For while too few who study beauty also study the true and the good, likewise too few who love truth and goodness bother to study beauty, what is most fitting, most becoming, and most lovely. But this sort of talk in a glossary is improper. Forgive me!

**provided**—[DJD] usually "provided that," it means: upon these terms; this stipulation being made. From "provide," meaning to procure beforehand; to get ready; to prepare; to furnish; to supply. Related in form to "providence," which means foresight; timely care; prudence; or the care of God over created things, divine superintendence.

[M5] from the Latin *pro-* and *-video*, meaning for and see, so a thing foreseen. Providence, be it God's, man's, or beast's, concerns foreseeing a need and furnishing what is needed ahead of time. Pity those who are blind to what has been and what needs to be provided.

# Q

**Quecámbia**—[M5] this wooly mammal's name is pronounced like so: kay-KAHM-bee-uh or queCÁMbia.

**queerly**—[DJD] particularly; oddly.

**quiver**—[DJD] 1. to quake; to play with a tremulous motion; to shiver; to shudder. 2. nimble; active. 3. a case of arrows.

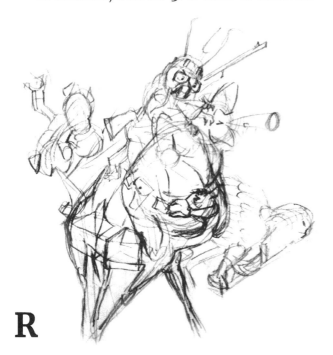

# R

**ransomed**—[WEB] past tense of "ransom," which means: 1. to redeem from captivity, servitude, punishment, or forfeit, by paying a price; to buy out of servitude or penalty; to rescue; to deliver; as, to ransom prisoners from an enemy. 2. to exact a ransom for, or a payment on.

**Rare**—[M5] pronounced just like it looks, though who has ever gotten to stare at the Rare?

**rebuffed**—[DJD] past tense of "rebuff," which means: to beat back; to oppose with sudden violence.

**reeds**—[DJD] 1. an hollow knotted stalk; which grows in wet ground. 2. a small pipe. The mighty poet John Milton says in *Paradise Lost* that the fiery cherubim, angels of heaven, are so wakeful that they would never become drowsy under the spell of the "Arcadian pipe, the pastoral reed / Of Hermes." 3. an arrow.

**refrain**—[WEB] 1. to hold back; to restrain; to keep within prescribed bounds; to curb; to govern. "His reason refraineth not his foul delight or talent" (Chaucer's *Parson's Tale*). 2. to abstain from. 3. to keep one's self from action or interference; to hold aloof; to forbear. 4. the burden of a song; a phrase or verse which recurs at the end of each of the separate stanzas or divisions of a poetic composition.

**regained**—[DJD] the past tense of "regain," which means: to recover; to gain anew. The majestic Milton writes of the need to speak truly in the face of the divorcing power of confusion, sin, error, or ignorance: "Hopeful to regain / Thy love, from thee I will not hide / What thoughts in my unquiet breast are risen."

**regal**—[DJD] royal, kingly.

**regurgitates**—[M5] when animals pour out digested food from their stomachs or gullets either to chew it again in their mouths, as cows do (and we call this rumination), or to feed it into the mouths of their young, as pelicans and Tanglis do.

**rehashed**—[WEB] the past tense of "rehash," meaning: to hash over again; to prepare or use again; as, to rehash old arguments. Relatedly, "hash" is a new mixture of old matter; a second preparation or exhibition.

   [M5] how we mix things truly matters.

**rehearse**—[DJD] 1. to repeat; to recite. 2. to relate; to tell.

   [M5] some poems, like "The Evol," are not worth memorizing or rehearsing; others, like "The Blug," "The Dally," "The Lundregun," "The Rare," or "To Be Like the Sillymede," are. And still others, like "The Jargontalky," "The Oominoos," "The Noble Myth of the Unraz, King of the Beasts," "The Double Vólle," and "The Zealion," are a sort of delightfully difficult memorization and rehearsal challenge!

replete—[DJD] full; completely filled; filled to exuberance.

repose—[WEB] 1. a lying at rest; sleep; rest; quiet. 2. rest of mind; tranquility; freedom from uneasiness; also, a composed manner or deportment.

roving—[WEB] the act of one who roves or wanders. To rove is to wander; to ramble; to go, move, or pass without certain direction in any manner, by sailing, walking, riding, flying, or otherwise. To rove can also mean to plow into ridges by turning the earth of two furrows together.

# S

Sandy Birch—[M5] see the entry for "birch" above.

sapling—[M5] these baby trees are called saplings because they suckle themselves on their own sap, because plants and all vegetative souls must bear a certain loneliness, but baby mammals are called nurslings because mammals are social by nature and their mothers do not leave them to a lonely world. I, for one, am glad to be a mammal, and once a nursling, rather than to be a tree, and so once a lonely sapling.

savannas—[WEB] a tract of level land covered with the vegetable growth usually found in a damp soil and warm climate, as grass or reeds, but destitute of trees.

scales—[DJD] 1. to climb as by ladders. 2. to measure or compare; to weigh. 3. to take off a thin lamina. 4. to pare off a surface. "If all the mountains were scaled, and the earth made even, the waters would not overflow the smooth surface" (Thomas Burnet's *Sacred Theory of the Earth, Containing an Account of the Original of the Earth and of all the General Changes which it hath already undergone, or is to undergo, till the Consummation of all Things*).

scholars—[DJD] 1. one who learns of a matter; a disciple. 2. a man of letters. 3. a pedant; a man of books. 4. one who has a lettered education. As Robert Shallow says, "By yea and no, sir. I dare say my cousin William is / a good scholar: he is at Oxford still, is he not?" (Shakespeare's 2 *Henry VI*).

science—[M5] it's best to be careful when someone says "this is science" or "I have a science," because all that mammal is really saying is "this is a body of knowledge" or "I have a body of knowledge." If someone says to you, "I have a body of knowledge," then you would, perhaps, raise an eyebrow and reply, "Well, perhaps you do, and perhaps you don't. It depends on whether the knowledge is really knowledge and whether you're an honest mammal. For you could be a fool or you could be a jerk, and in both (or either) cases, I can't trust your work." That said, we all need good science, good knowledge, of all sorts (languages, geometry, history, zoology, ethics), for as Shakespeare, whom we call The Bard, wrote, "Ignorance is the curse of God, / Knowledge the wing wherewith we fly to heaven. . . ." The Bard is right, of course, for how can we die well and with a good conscience, if we don't live well with a good science.

**scrunch**—[WEB] to crunch; to grind.

[M5] have you ever had to scrunch yourself into a tiny space you never thought would fit you? It's an absurd word that sounds like its meaning. See the entry for "Hai-chus" above to learn more of such words.

**secretes**—[WEB] to separate from the blood and elaborate by the process of secretion; to elaborate and emit as a secretion.

[M5] all mammals, mythical or not, are amazing! Their mothers make milk from their very own blood, and generously give it to their babies, boarlets, calfs, colts, crias, cubs, farrows, fawns, fillies, foals, infants, joeys, kids, kits, kittens, lambs, lambkins, leverets, piglets, puggles, pups, porcupettes, shoats, stots, and whelps. See the entry for "Mammals" above.

**seeped**—[WEB] the past tense of "seep," meaning to run or soak through fine pores and interstices; to ooze.

**senses**—[WEB] 1. a faculty, possessed by animals, of perceiving external objects by means of impressions made upon certain sensory organs of the body, or of perceiving changes in the condition of the body; as, the senses of sight, smell, hearing, taste, and touch. 2. perception through the intellect; apprehension; recognition; understanding; discernment; appreciation. As the witty poet and politician Sir Philip Sydney once wrote, "This Basilius, having the quick sense of a lover." 3. sound perception and reasoning; correct judgment; good mental capacity; understanding; also, that which is sound, true, or reasonable; rational meaning. As the senseless Pistol declares, "He speaks sense" (Shakespeare's *Merry Wives of Windsor*). 4. meaning; import; signification; as,

the true sense of words or phrases; the sense of a remark. 5. moral perception or appreciation. "Some are so hardened in wickedness as to have no sense of the most friendly offices" (L' Estrange's fable of *The Mouse and the Kite*).

[M5] in Cervantes' famous novel *Don Quixote*, the poor, silly squire, Sancho Panza, says that if he leaves Don Quixote's side for even a second, he'd be "almost frightened out of [his] seven senses." What a wise little man to see we have more than only the five bodily senses!

**severs**—[DJD] 1. to part by violence from the rest. 2. to divide; to part; to force asunder. 3. to separate; to put in different orders or places. 4. to disjoin; to disunite. 4. to make a separation; to make a partition.

**shafts**—[DJD] 1. an arrow. 2. a narrow, deep, perpendicular pit. 3. any thing strait; the spire of a church.

**shroud**—[DJD] 1. a shelter; a cover. 2. the dress of the dead; a winding-sheet. "The screech owl screeching loud, / Puts the wretch that lies in woe / In remembrance of a shroud" (Shakespeare's *Midsummer Night's Dream*). 3. the sail ropes or sometimes the sails themselves. As Alexander Pope so hauntingly wrote, "He summons strait his denizens of air; / The lucid squadrons round the sails repair: / Soft o'er the shrouds aerial whispers breathe, / That seemed but zephyrs" (*The R. of the Lock: An Heroi-Comical Poem*).

**shuns**—[DJD] to avoid; to decline; to endeavor to escape; to eschew.

[M5] the statesman Thomas More wrote a short poem in Latin about two beggars, the last lines of which can be translated like this into English: "The love that binds our heartstrings / shuns the high castles of proudest kings, / but in the poor man's humble hut, it reigns."

**Sillymede**—[M5] "SIL-ly-mede" rhymes with "centipede." This mythical mammal sounds like two words: first, the word "silly," and then the word "mead," which, Dr. Johnson tells us, means either particularly watery ground, as in "meadow," or a drink made with water and honey, like the sort served in mighty Herot, the hall of King Hrothgar, in the Old English poem *Beowulf*. Or it sounds like "meed," which means a reward or payment, like the kind that Viking heroes such as Beowulf would receive for defeating monsters or dragons. In fact—it's silly to think!—many a hero in Herot hall was given mead for his meed!

**simile**—[DJD] a comparison by which any thing is illustrated or aggrandized.

[M5] a comparison using "like" or "as," as when one says, "A metaphor is like a simile" or "a donkey is like an onager as an ass is like a kiang."

**skirts**—[DJD] to border; to run along the edge.

**slunk**—[DJD] 1. past tense of "slink," which means: 1. to sneak; to steal out of the way. "He after Eve seduced, unminded slunk / Into the woods fast by" (Milton's *Paradise Lost*). 2. a base word meaning to miscarry.

**song**—[DJD] any thing modulated in the utterance. 2. a poem modulated by the voice; a ballad. 3. a poem; a lay; strain. 4. poetry; poesy. 5. notes of birds.

**sonnet**—[DJD] 1. a short poem consisting of fourteen lines, of which the rhymes are adjusted by a particular rule. It is not very suitable to the English language, and has not been used by any man of eminence since Milton. 2. a small poem. "Let us into the city presently, / To sort some gentlemen well skilled in music; / I have a sonnet that will serve the turn" (Shakespeare's *Two Gentlemen of Verona*).

**sopped**—[WEB] from "sop," which means:

1. anything steeped, or dipped and softened, in any liquid; especially, something dipped in broth or liquid food, and intended to be eaten. 2. anything given to pacify.

**soul**—[WEB] 1. the spiritual, rational, and immortal part in man; that part of man which enables him to think, and which renders him a subject of moral government; sometimes, in distinction from the higher nature, or spirit, of man, the so-called animal soul, that is, the seat of life, the sensitive affections and phantasy, exclusive of the voluntary and rational powers; sometimes, in distinction from the mind, the moral and emotional part of man's nature, the seat of feeling, in distinction from intellect; sometimes, the intellect only; the understanding; the seat of knowledge, as distinguished from feeling. "The eyes of our souls only then begin to see, when our bodily eyes are closing" (Rev. William Law's *A Serious Call to a Devout and Holy Life*). 2. the seat of real life or vitality; the source of action; the animating or essential part. 3. the leader; the inspirer; the moving spirit; the heart; as, the soul of an enterprise; an able general is the soul of his army. 4. energy; courage; spirit; fervor; affection, or any other noble manifestation of the heart or moral nature; inherent power or goodness. 5. a human being; a person; as, poor soul. "As cold water to a thirsty soul, so is good tidings from a far country" (Prv 25:25). "God forbid so many simple souls / Should perish by the sword!" (Shakespeare's *2 Henry VI*). 6. pure or disembodied spirit.

[M5] in the ancient Greek philosopher Plato's famous dialogue, the *Phaedo*, his teacher Socrates argues how irrational it would be to deny that we humans, unlike all the other mammals, have immortal souls. In fact, death, he teaches, is none other than the separation of the body from the soul.

**South Dakota**—[M5] the fortieth state to enter the union of the United States of America, this land of allies bears the motto: "Under God the people rule." And so they do, from Mt. Rushmore to the Badlands to Big Sioux Falls.

**spires**—[DJD] 1. a curve line; anything wreathed or contorted; a curl; a twist; a wreath. "A dragon's fiery form belied the god, / Sublime on radiant spires he rode" (Dryden's *Alexander's Feast, or The Power of Music*). 2. any thing growing up to a taper; a round pyramid, so called because a line drawn round and round in less and less circles, would be a spire; a steeple.

[M5] though it would be very fine if it were so, "spires" does not come from the Latin word *spirare*, which means to breathe and which is where we get the word "inspiration," like that of the Muse for the poets or like that of the Spirit for the prophets. See the "Muses" entry above.

**spite**—[WEB] 1. ill-will or hatred toward another, accompanied with the disposition to irritate, annoy, or thwart; petty malice; grudge; rancor; despite. 2. vexation; chagrin; mortification. 3. to be angry at; to hate; to treat maliciously; to try to injure or thwart; to fill with spite; to offend; to vex.

**stalactites**—[M5] stalag*mites* are the spires in caves that come up from the floor, but stala*ctites* are the spires that come down from the ceiling in caves. Perhaps this batty little rhyme will help you keep them straight in your head: "Bats hold *tight* to the ceiling or / they *might* get stuck on the cold, hard floor!"

**steed**—[DJD] a horse for state or war.

**stews**—[DJD] to seeth anything in a slow moist heat; to be seethed in a slow moist heat.

[WEB] to boil slowly; to cook in a little liquid.

**stoops**—[WEB] 1. to bend the upper part of the body downward and forward; to bend or lean forward; to incline forward in standing or walking; to assume habitually a bent position. 2. to yield; to submit; to bend, as by compulsion; to assume a position of humility or subjection. 3. to descend from rank or dignity; to condescend. 4. to come down as a hawk does on its prey; to pounce; to souse; to swoop. 5. to sink when on the wing; to alight.

**strong-willed**—[M5] a strong will can be good if you will a good thing, but if you will whatever you want and won't listen to anyone or thing, then "strong-willed" is a nice way to say you're as stubborn as a mule.

**subsumed**—[WEB] the past tense of "subsume," which means to take up into or under, as individual under species, species under genus, or particular under universal; to place (any one cognition) under another as belonging to it; to include under something else.

**suits**—[DJD] 1. to fit; to adapt to something else. 2. to be fitted to; to become. 3. to dress; to clothe. "I'll disrobe me / Of these Italian weeds, and suit myself / As does a Briton peasant" (Shakespeare's *Cymbeline*). 4. to agree; to accord.

**sun-kissed**—[M5] when the light of the sun shines on something so that it beams with life and light, the way we mammals beam when someone kisses us.

**sups**—[WEB] 1. to eat the evening meal; to take supper.

**sustain**—[DJD] 1. to bear; to prop; to hold up. 2. to support; to keep from sinking under evil. 3. to maintain; to keep. 4. to help; to relieve; to assist. 5. to bear without yielding; to endure. 6. to suffer; to bear as inflicted.

swear—[M5] to swear an oath is a very serious thing, and sadly many mammals do so vainly. Dear Tully (that's Marcus Tullius Cicero to his acquaintances) describes swearing an oath this way in *On Duties*: "An oath is an assurance backed by religious sanctity; and a solemn promise given, as before God as one's witness, must be kept. . . . He who violates his oath violates Good Faith [*Fidem*]." In the New Testament, the Apostle and Evangelist Matthew wrote down the words of Jesus about swearing vain oaths: "But I tell you that you should not bind yourselves by any oath at all: not by heaven, for heaven is God's throne; nor by earth, for earth is the footstool under his feet; nor by Jerusalem, for it is the city of the great king. And thou shalt not swear by thy own head, for thou hast no power to turn a single hair of it white or black. Let your word be Yes for Yes, and No for No; whatever goes beyond this, comes of evil."

sycophantic—[DJD] flattering; parasitical.

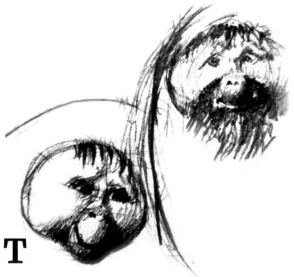

**T**

tale—[DJD] 1. a narrative; a story. Commonly a slight or petty account of some trifling or fabulous incident: as, a tale of a tub. 2. oral relation. 3. information; disclosure of anything secret.

Tanglis—[M5] thankfully, this mammal's name is easy enough to say. TANGlis is "TANG-" which rhymes with "sang" and "-lis" which rhymes with "kiss." "Tang" and "gliss" smushed together makes "Tanglis."

Texarkana—[M5] a city split in two by the border between the Lone Star State of Texas, the twenty-eighth to enter the union of the United States of America, and Arkansas, the twenty-fifth state to enter the union, with its hot springs and south winds. And not only is the city split in two, so too is its name!

theme—[DJD] 1. a subject on which one speaks or writes. 2. a short dissertation written by children on any topic. 3. the original word whence others are derived.
   [M5] what, really, is the Evol's theme?

thoughtless—[DJD] 1. airy; gay; dissipated. 2. negligent; careless. 3. stupid; dull.

thronging—[DJD] 1. crowding; coming in tumultuous multitudes. 2. oppressing with crowds or tumults. "I have seen the dumb men throng to see him and the blind / To hear him speak" (Shakespeare's *Coriolanus*).

thrum—[WEB] to play rudely or monotonously on a stringed instrument with the fingers; to strum. 2. hence, to make a monotonous drumming noise; as, to thrum on a table.
   [M5] thrumming, in that monotonous whirring way, is the sound of the cicada, on a hot summer's day.

toil—[DJD] 1. to labor; perhaps originally, to labor in tillage. 2. to work at; to weary; to overlabor. "Then, toiled with works of war, retired himself / To Italy" (Shakespeare's *Richard II*).

tolling—[DJD] 1. paying or taking a toll or tallage. 2. sounding as a single bell. "The first bringer of unwelcome news / Hath but a losing office; and his tongue sounds ever after as a sullen bell, / Remembered tolling a departing friend" (Shakespeare's *2 Henry IV*).

**tomb**—[WEB] 1. a pit in which the dead body of a human being is deposited; a grave; a sepulcher. "Methinks I see thee, now thou art below, / As one dead in the bottom of a tomb: / Either my eyesight fails, or thou look'st pale" (Shakespeare's *The Tragedy of Romeo and Juliet*). 2. a house or vault, formed wholly or partly in the earth, with walls and a roof, for the reception of the dead. 3. a monument erected to enclose the body and preserve the name and memory of the dead.

**tongue**—[M5] the sense of taste comes in through our tongues, but words too are sent to the ear by more than just our lungs.

**topsy-turvy**—[DJD] with the bottom upward, perhaps from one's top being in the turf. "If we without his help can make a head / To push against the kingdom; with his help / We shall o'erturn it topsy-turvey down" (Shakespeare's *1 Henry IV*). "God told man what was good, but the devil surnamed it evil, and thereby turned the world topsy-turvy, and brought a new chaos upon the whole creation" (Robert South's *Sermons*). "But a broomstick, perhaps you will say, is an Emblem of a Tree standing on its Head; And pray what is man but a topsy-turvy creature? His Animal Faculties perpetually mounted on his Rational; his Head where his Heels should be, groveling on the Earth" (Jonathan Swift's *A Meditation upon a Broom-stick*).

**totter**—[WEB] 1. to shake so as to threaten a fall; to vacillate; to be unsteady; to stagger; as, an old man totters with age. 2. to shake; to reel; to lean; to waver.

**touch**—[DJD] 1. the sense of feeling. "The spiders touch how exquisitely fine! / Feels at each thread, and lives along the line" (Alexander Pope's *Essay on Man*) 2. to reach with any thing, so as that there be no space between the thing reached and the thing brought to it. 3. to affect; to relate to. 4. to censure; to animadvert upon. 5. to infect; to seize slightly. 6. to bite; to wear; to have an effect on. 7. to strike a musical instrument. 8. to influence by impulse; to impel forcibly.

[M5] the basest of the five senses, meant only for perceiving exclusively physical things, and that with the least clarity. That is, of the five senses, it is the worst for knowing the truth of things, but the best for giving some mammal you know and love a hug! In the same vein, consider this translated or modernized version of the sharp-eyed poet John Godfrey Saxe:

*The Blind Men and the Elephant*
A Hindu Fable.

Six scientific men began
A study they'd designed.
They went to see the Elephant
(Though all of them were blind),
And hoped, by crude sensation,
to satisfy their minds.

The *First* approached the Elephant,
And happening to fall
Against his broad and sturdy side,
At once began to bawl:
"By Charles!—why this Elephant
Is very like a wall!"

The *Second*, feeling of the tusk,
Cried: "Ho!—what have we here
So very round and smooth and sharp?
To me it's mighty clear
This wonder of an Elephant
Is very like a spear!"

The *Third* approached the animal,
And happening to take
The squirming trunk within his hands,
Thus boldly up and spake:
"I see," said he, "the Elephant
Is very like a snake!"

The *Fourth* reached out his eager hand,
And felt about the knee.
"What most this wondrous beast is like

Is mighty plain," said he;
"It's clear enough the Elephant
Is very like a tree!"

The *Fifth*, who chanced to touch the ear,
Said: "Even the blindest man
Can tell what this resembles most;
Deny the fact who can,
This marvel of an Elephant
Is very like a fan!"

The *Sixth* no sooner had begun
About the beast to grope,
Than, seizing on the swinging tail
That fell within his scope,
"I see," said he, "the Elephant
Is very like a rope!"

And so each scientific man
Disputed loud and long,
Each in his own opinion
Exceeding stiff and strong,
Though each was partly in the right,
And all were in the wrong!

**touchingly**—[DJD] with feeling emotion; in a pathetic manner.

[M5] in the liberal art of rhetoric, *pathos* is what is known as one of the three rhetorical appeals, namely that appeal which touchingly causes the listener to be moved in feeling toward what you say. The other two rhetorical appeals are *logos*, the logic or reasoning of what you say, and *ethos*, the character you have to present, which might induce a listener to trust you.

**trek**—[WEB] the act of trekking; a traveling; a journey; a migration.

**troglodytic**—[WEB] of or pertaining to a troglodyte, or dweller in caves.

[M5] this word rhymes with "critic."

**tropic**—[DJD] the line at which the sun turns back, of which the North has the tropic of Cancer, and the South has the tropic of Capricorn.

[WEB] 1. one of the two parallels of terrestrial latitude corresponding to the celestial tropics, and called by the same

names. 2. the region lying between these parallels of latitude, or near them on either side.

[M5] the tropic region contains, unsurprisingly, the . . . tropical rainforests, which are wondrous lands and magnificent sources of life for this world.

**turn**—[DJD] 1. to change as to the posture of the body, or direction of the look. 2. to form; to shape. 3. to change to another opinion, or party, worse or better; to convert or to pervert.

[M5] from the ancient Greek, the word is *protreptic*, or the reorienting—the turning—of one's mind and soul from the cruel thorns of ignorance and fashion to the fairest fields of truth and goodness.

**tu-wit tu-who**—[M5] what owls used to say, back when they knew a thing or tu.

# U

**unassayable**—[DJD] unable to attempt, unable to attack or trouble; unable to make a trial or experiment of; unable to examine; in law, when one is unable to officially examine the measures and weights being used as standard.

**unctuous**—[DJD] fat; clammy; oily.
[M5] "unctuous" sounds like the last part of "rambunctious."

**undertake**—[DJD] 1. to assume any business; to venture; to hazard. 2. to promise; to stand bound to some condition.

**undulate**—[M5] ordinarily a verb, here it is used as an adjective, identical in meaning to "undulated," which, the WEB tells us, means resembling, or in the nature of, waves; having a wavy surface; undulatory. One delightful thing about poetry is that it has a special freedom of expression, in which the normal rules of grammar only sometimes apply.

**unfenced**—[M5] without a fence.

**unfortunately**—[DJD] unhappily; without good luck.
[M5] the word implies some suffering at the hands of fortune. Shakespeare once warned that what "we profanely term our fortunes," perhaps also our misfortunes, are "the provision of the power above, / Fitted and shaped just to that strength of nature / Which we are born with."

**unintended**—[M5] without intention or purpose; unmindfully; carelessly.

**unloving**—[M5] read the entry above for "love" and then imagine the opposite of having love.

**unnatural**—[M5] read the entries above for "natural" and "nature" and then imagine the opposite of those. Mammals love nature too much to like this word.

**unsubstantial**—[DJD] not solid; not palpable. As poor, contemn'd (that is, hated), yet still esperant (that is, hopeful) Edgar declares in Shakespeare's *King Lear*, when Edgar had lost all his worldly and material possessions, "Yet better thus, and known to be contemn'd, / Than still contemn'd and flatter'd. To be worst, / The lowest and most dejected thing of fortune, / Stands still in esperance, lives not in fear. / The lamentable change is from the best; / The worst returns to laughter. Welcome then, / Thou unsubstantial air that I embrace! / The wretch that thou hast blown unto the worst / Owes nothing to thy blasts."

**updrafts**—[M5] 1. a draft of air, on its way up, of course!

**urnastic**—[M5] of or pertaining to the manner or character of the Urnaz; as or associated with the Urnaz. See entry for "Urnaz" just below.

**Urnaz**—[M5] there are two ways to pronounce this word, the American way or the urnastic way. Let me spell them out for you: (1) the American way: say "Ur-" as in "hurt" and "-naz" as in "jazz"—URnaz. (2) The urnastic way: say "Ur-" as in "doer" or "grandeur," and say "-naz" like the last part of "applause"—OORnahs . . . or URnaz.

**utter**—[DJD] 1. situated on the outside, or remote from the center. 2. placed without any compass; out of place. 3. extreme; excessive; utmost. 4. complete; irrevocable. 5. to speak; to pronounce; to express.

# V

**vale**—[DJD] a low ground; a valley; a place between two hills. It is a poetical word.

**Vaquitas**—[M5] my new-found friend, Diane Glim, a leading Vaquita conservationist and the former president of the American Cetacean Society can tell us about this marvelous mammal: "The smallest of all cetaceans, as well as the most endangered, the vaquita porpoise lives only in the northern section of the Sea of Cortez, off Baja California, Mexico. It was not until the 1950s that a chance find of a vaquita skull led to the naming of this new species of porpoise, la vaquita. In the sixty years since its discovery, the vaquita population has plummeted, to the dangerous low of less than thirty in existence in 2018. The primary cause of decline is by incidental catches in gillnets that are set for shrimp and a highly lucrative fish, the totoaba. Although reserves and fishing restrictions have been implemented to save the vaquita from extinction, the value of the totoaba swim bladder (called "Money Maw") in Chinese medicine has made the risks of fishing for totoaba and the resulting near-extinction of the vaquita unimportant to far too many. For more information, please visit www.vivavaquita.org."

Diane and I hope this babiest of all the baby whales (or cetaceans really) does not slip forever into myth! The mammals of this world are in our care, but once lost, the world is sadly more bare—and all because we human mammals couldn't be bothered to care.

**vastness**—[DJD] 1. immensity; enormous greatness.

**ventures**—[DJD] 1. to dare. 2. to run a hazard. 3. to engage in; or make attempts without any security of success, upon mere hope. 4. to expose to hazard; to put or send on a venture.

[M5] don't forget the wise old proverb: nothing ventured, nothing gained.

**verse**—[DJD] a line consisting of a certain succession of sounds, and number of syllables. 2. a section or paragraph of a book. 3. poetry; lays; metrical language. 4. a piece of poetry.

**visions**—[WEB] 1. that which is seen; an object of sight. 2. especially, that which is seen otherwise than by the ordinary sight, or the rational eye; a supernatural, prophetic, or imaginary sight; an apparition; a phantom; a specter; as, the visions of Isaiah. Theologically, the Beatific Vision, the immediate sight of God in heaven.

[M5] as the knowing American author Nathaniel Hawthorne wrote in his short story, "The Artist of the Beautiful," in *Mosses from an Old Manse, and Other Stories*: "Owen Warland felt the impulse to give external reality to his ideas as irresistibly as any of the poets or painters who have arrayed the world in a dimmer and fainter beauty, imperfectly copied from the richness of their visions."

**Vólle**—[M5] this mammal's name rhymes with "Nólle" and "okay," but stress it like VOL-le, okay? And I'll tell you something more: when like the Vólle you can't decide, and so you'd like to run and hide, then wish and pray you could be turned by some fiery guide, like father Virgil helped dear Dante's stride, when he stood and froze, a heart divided woefully, in Dante's *Divine Comedy*.

# W

**wallah**—[M5] in the mythical language spoken in the Inowallah's tropical forest, "wallah" is the plural of "wall" and also part of the plaintive cry of the Inowallah directed at wayfarers: "Inowallah wallah way." Augustine

126

of Hippo gave sermons calling man a wayfarer, or in Latin "*viator,*" passing through this life to the next. See the entries above for "death" and "soul."

**water-bound**—[M5] on first inspection from the shore, those Tanglis appear for all the world to be meant only for the water, bound or stuck, in the waves for all time. Yet they are meant for life beyond those watery bounds. Once we see their amazing efforts to climb, the power for which lies hidden in their heavy nature, those seeming boundaries give way to a further peak for those delightfully ridiculous mythical mammals.

**weir**—[WEB] 1. a fence of stakes, brushwood, or the like, set in a stream, tideway, or inlet of the sea, for taking fish. 2. a dam in a river to stop and raise the water, for the purpose of conducting it to a mill, forming a fish pond, or the like.

**whate'er**—[M5] to fit the meter of a line, poets often contract their words. "Whatever" is a three-syllable word, and that just wouldn't do. So I clipped it to "whate'er," and now it's only two. Poets call these little contractions syncope. 'Tis a thing oft done o'er the many hast'ning years, to syncopate our verses, howe'er it causes tears.

**wheeling**—[DJD] 1. turning on an axis. 2. revolving; having a rotatory motion; turning; having vicissitudes. 3. fetching a compass. "Spies / Held me in chase, that I was forc'd to wheel / Three or four miles about" (Shakespeare's *Coriolanus*). 4. rolling forward.

**whimsy**—[WEB] a whim; a freak; a capricious notion, a fanciful or odd conceit. "These days! where e'en th' extravagance of poetry / Is at a loss for figures to express / Men's folly, whimsies, and inconstancy, / And by a faint description make them less"

(Swift's "Ode to the Athenian Society").

**willy-nilly**—[M5] if you are willy-nilly, you both will something but also seem to not will it, or nill it. You are "like a man to double business bound," as Shakespeare put it. In fact, the Latin vulgarism, *nolens volens,* or *volens nolens,* was once a commonplace way for an English speaker to say, "either way" or "one way or another" or "take it or leave it" or "I'm undecided." This ancient Latin pairing comes from the *Epistles* of Seneca, but Augustine of Hippo made much of the phrase as well. These two great minds were, after all, the so-called discoverers of the human will and the fallen will, respectively. Or so we might say, willy-nilly.

**wily**—[DJD] cunning; sly; full of stratagem; fraudulent.

[M5] there is a fable of Aesop, retold by the Rev. Samuel Lysons, which I reproduce here:

*The Serpent and the Man:*

A little child that was playing in a nice green field accidently trod upon a serpent. The venomous beast, full of fury, turned round and bit the poor infant, with its poisonous fangs, so that it died immediately. The father of the child, in an agony of grief, took a weapon in his hand, and, pursuing the serpent, struck at it before it could reach its hole and cut off a piece of its tail: but it nevertheless escaped wounded to its retreat. The next day, hoping by a stratagem to be able to destroy the reptile entirely, he brought a mixture of meal, honey, and salt to its hole, and invited it to come out and partake of the presents he had brought, with the view of effecting a reconciliation. But he was unable to decoy the wily creature, who only hissed out more deadly threatenings of hostility from within its lurking place, saying, "In vain you attempt a reconciliation, for as long as the memory of the dead child on one side, and the mangled tail subsists on the other, it is impossible for us to be at peace with each other."

There will always be enmity between the father and that wily serpent. But for that poor and woeful father, it is too late to warn his simple son with the words of Matthew's gospel, to take care to learn the ways of that worldly, subtle serpent: "Be ye therefore wise as serpents and simple as doves" (Mt 10:16).

**wisdom**—[DJD] sapience; the power of judging rightly. "'Tis much he dares, / And to that dauntless temper of his mind, / He hath a wisdom that doth guide his valour / To act in safety" (Shakespeare's *Macbeth*). "Wisdom and fortune combating together, / If that the former dare what it can, / No chance may shake it" (Shakespeare's *Antony and Cleopatra*).

[M5] Seneca, the Roman philosopher, statesman, and playwright, spoke of wisdom and the liberal arts to his famous friend, the poet and official Lucilius, "Hence you see why 'liberal studies' are so called: it is because they are studies worthy of a free-born gentleman. But there is only one really liberal study,—that which gives man his liberty. It is the study of wisdom, and that is lofty, brave, and great-souled."

**wonder**—[DJD] 1. admiration; astonishment; amazement; surprise caused by something unusual or unexpected. "What is he, whose griefs / Bear such an emphasis? whose phrase or sorrow / Conjure the wand'ring stars, and makes them stand / Like wonder-wounded hearers" (Shakespeare's *Hamlet*). 2. cause of wonder; a strange thing; something more or greater than can be expected. "Lo, a wonder strange! / Of every beast, and bird, and insect small

/ Came sevens, and pairs" (Milton's *Paradise Lost*). 3. anything mentioned with wonder. "And a kind of network, and chain work wreathed together with wonderful art" (1 Kgs 7:17).

[M5] the ancient Greek philosopher Aristotle said this of wonder: "For it is owing to their wonder that men both now begin and at first began to philosophize; they wondered originally at the obvious difficulties, then advanced little by little and stated difficulties about the greater matters, about the phenomena of the moon and those of the sun, and about the stars and about the genesis of the universe. And a man who is puzzled and wonders thinks himself ignorant, whence even the lover of myth is in a sense a lover of Wisdom, for the myth is composed of wonders."

**Wooly-Quilled Quecámbia**—[M5] see the "Quecámbia" entry above.

**worm**—[DJD] 1. a small harmless serpent that lives in the earth. "God's wrong is most of all. / If thou hadst fear'd to break an oath by Him, / The unity the king thy brother made / Had not been broken, nor my brother slain: / If thou hadst fear'd to break an oath by Him, / The imperial metal, circling now thy brow, / Had graced the tender temples of my child, / And both the princes had been breathing here, / Which now, two tender playfellows to dust, / Thy broken faith hath made a prey for worms. / What canst thou swear by now?" (Shakespeare's *History of Richard III*). 2. a poisonous serpent. 3. animal bred in the body. 4. animal that spins silk. 5. grubs that gnaw wood and furniture. 6. something tormenting. As Queen Margaret curses the would-be tyrant king of England: "If heaven have any grievous plague in store / Exceeding those that I can wish upon thee, / O, let them keep it till thy sins be ripe, / And then hurl down their indignation / On thee, the troubler of the poor world's peace! / The worm of conscience still begnaw thy soul! / Thy friends suspect for traitors while thou livest, / And take deep traitors for thy dearest friends! / No sleep close up that deadly eye of thine, / Unless it be whilst some tormenting dream / Affrights thee with a hell of ugly devils!" (Shakespeare's *Richard III*).

[M5] which of these is the gross kind? Which is the kind used for fishing and composting?

**wrought**—[DJD] effected; performed; produced; caused; actuated; formed; guided; managed.

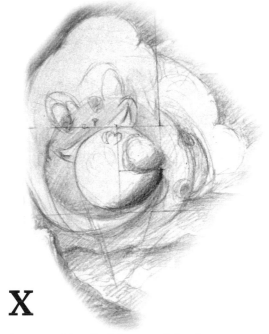

# X

**Xero**—[M5] this mythical mammal's name is said exactly like the number: zero.

# Y

**Y-It**—[M5] "Why" and "It"—Y-It.

# Z

**Zealion**—[M5] this mammal is *not* pronounced like "Zeal-" and "-ion," or at least not said aloud that way for the poem's sake. Better to pronounce it like the letter "Z," plus "lion," the maned mammal and king of the beasts. So ZEE-lion, or Zealion.

**zealous**—[DJD] ardently passionate in any cause. "We should be not only devout towards God, but zealous towards men; endeavoring by all prudent means to recover them out of those snares of the devil, whereby they are taken captive" (Eaton College provost Richard Allestree's *The Causes of the Decay of Christian Piety*).

[M5] one mythical mammal, the Dumb Ox of Aquino, said something like this about zeal: "A man is said to be zealous when on behalf of his friend it's understood, that he zealously repels whatever malice may be said or done against his dear friend's good."

**zoologic**—[WEB] of or pertaining to zoology, or the science of animals.

**zoology**—[DJD] a treatise concerning living creatures.

Note: All works reproduced or cited in this glossary are in the public domain. I would, nevertheless, like to thank the good people at johnsonsdictionaryonline.com for their digital edition of Dr. Samuel Johnson's *Dictionary of the English Language* (1755). I would also like to thank Oxford University Press and the Oxford English Dictionary teams for their guidance.

# Regarding Those Big Black Letters

Below, behold an apt and lovely list of alphabetical alliterations, which were depicted deliberately on or around all the tall, big, black letters lain atop all the mythical mammal poems. Perhaps there are additional alliterations as well, which are unknown and unlisted?

*(Spoiler Alert!)*

**A**—An Anguished Amber Ango Arduously Aiming Another Archer's Arrow at an Auburn Apple

**B**—The Blug Blithely Blowing Bubbles with a Brass Bubble Blower Beneath a Beautiful Blue Butterfly

**C**—The Colvaino Chomping Chocolate Chip Cookies and Coffee-Colored Cobblestones and Coughing a Carbonous Cloud

**D**—The Ditch-Digging Dally Dangling in a Dane's Doublet and Dislocating a Dozen Dandelions and a Detached Daffodil in a Dirt Depression

**E**—The Evol Eating or Evacuating Eight Ebony, Eggplant, and Ecru Easter Eggs

**F**—The Fáh-la-las Flashing Floridly, Framing the Letter F and Floating Far off

**G**—A Gray Gallant Giving Guidance to a Growth of Green Grapes Germinating from the Ground

**H**—A Hairy Hai-chu Holding a Hachiwari upon which Hangs Heliotrope

**I**—Inowallahs In Intertwining Ivy Inking an Illuminated Image Including an Interesting Insignia

**J**—A Jabbering Jargontalky Juggling a Jaguar, Jackal, and Juvenile Jack Russell Terrier while Jiggling a Jack-in-the-box

**K**—The Kalondahres Keeping Knots of Kittens and Kitties also a Knight and a King

**L**—The Lurking Lundregun Lit by Lightening below a Little Lug with a Lowered Lifesaver on a Line

**M**—A Mixxy and a Moth admiring a Milk Moon's Midpoint Mirrored in a Memorable Mere

**N**—The Nólle Numbering Nine Nesting Nightingales Nibbling Nightcrawlers

**O**—One Oryx Offering Obeisance to One Oominoos

**P**—A Pillow-Padded Porcupine Perseveres Peacefully as the Plee Pesters a Peeved, Plump hippopotamus

**Q**—The Quecambia Quartering Quinoa on a Quilt for a Quartet of Querulous Quails

**R**—The Rare Reaching from a Rickety Rounded Rung for a Red *De Re Publica* in a Rare books Reading Room

**S**—Six Sleepy Sheep Springing over a Stone Stockade as the Sky Shifts from a Setting Sun to Some Sparkling Starlight

**T**—Two Tubby Tanglis Tots Tackling a Teeter-Totter after Trying a Toy Top

**U**—The Urnaz Under Umbrellas Ushered Upstairs between Unicorns on Unicycles with Umber Undertones

**V**—A Vaquita Viewing Various Verses in Vivid and Vibrant Vegetation above a Viable Vaquitita

**W**—A Winged Vólle Wound Within the W While Warring With the Wee-Winged one in Withering Wheat, While the Wide-Winged one Windily Whaps its Wings, Wafting the Waves of a Wonderfully Wild Waterfall

**X**—An X-Ray in Xenon of an exiting Xero and other taxonomical examples

**Y**—Y-It's Yo-yos

**Z**—The Zany Zealion before a bronze Zoo of Mr. Mehan's Mildly Amusing Mythical Mammals! Can you find zem all?

*O wonder!*
*How many goodly creatures are there here!*
—Miranda, Shakespeare's *Tempest* 5.1.181–82

# "I Spy with My Little Eye"

Well, you've nearly made it to the end, so you must be a curious and studious reader, my friend! Here is a little surprise: the paintings, A through Z, are packed with little treasures put there by Mr. Folley and by me. If you are one who sits and stoops in books, you too can spy these dodgy little details, one-by-one, thrown in mostly just for fun. What follows is a mysterious list with no answer key. For many below, you may have to consult the world beyond this book, and then come back to take a look.

Happy hunting! Look around! Feel free!

## Easy Finds:

-A critically endangered and impossibly cute vaquita calf, which is about the size of a loaf of bread (*Phocoena sinus*).
-Five microphones.
-A day moon, or two.
-More than half of a black bear.
-A microscope and a telescope in the same painting.
-The now extinct New Zealand Laughing Owl (*Sceloglaux albifacies*).
-One lighthouse, namely the Lighthouse of San Felipe.
-Duo of inkwells.
-Duo of umbrellas.
-Scissors, three pair.
-Not quite a third, much greener umbrella.
-Eight Easter eggs.
-Eggs, the unpainted kind, at least five.
-Disruptive paper airplane.
-Single sheep, standing and asleep.
-Ear-horns, three of them throughout.
-Very dark, half-hidden set of silent spurs.
-Eyeglasses, eight at least.
-Nests, two in number.
-Lightening.
-One badminton racquet.
-Very unusual, wooden shoes (called geta).
-Excited herd of this vulnerable species: the Syrian or golden hamster (*Mesocricetus auratus*).

## Harder Finds:

-Mt. Grossglockner, the tallest mountain in
　　Austria.
-A mighty tree from the ruins of the temple of
　　Siem Reap, Cambodia.
-Yellow chalk.
-Traces of the now extinct St. Helena giant
　　hoopoe bird (*Upupa antaios*).
-Hidden skull.
-Endangered saiga antelope (*Saiga tatarica*),
　　sort of.
-Four seasons in one painting.
-A pagoda.
-Monument Valley.
-Barber's poles, sort of.
-Magnificent frigate birds (*Fregata magnificens*).
-One Assyrian lamassu or bull, a most ancient mythical mammal.
-Ronda's famous Puente Nuevo in Andalusia, Spain.
-Endangered Axolotl or Mexican Salamander (*Ambystoma mexicanum*), sort of.

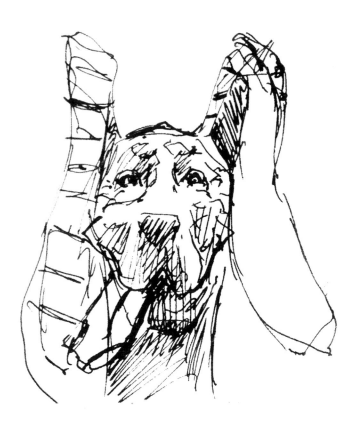

## Still Harder Finds:

-Three Loeb editions, sort of.
-Most of a gibbon.
-A few Hungarian puli dogs, sort of.
-The blooming bottle trees of Socotra Island in the Indian Ocean, sort of.
-Treasury of Delphi.
-The Mixxy hiding in five of the other letters' illustrations.
-A caduceus, or two, or three, or four, or five . . .
-Christ's Church College, Oxford, where Lewis Carroll taught.
-Lewis Carrol's White Rabbit, after the fashion of the original illustrations by John
　　Tenniel.
-One hidden whirling dervish.
-Very strange letters from Lewis Carroll's secret language.
-Reading, in braille.
-Letters from the alphabet of the Utopians.
-N. C. Wyeth's illustration of the Lady of the Lake, sort of.
-The Fibonacci Sequence, illustrated.
-The threatened Totoaba Fish (Totoaba macdonaldi).
-The Writing Machine of Laputa from Jonathan Swift's *Gulliver's Travels*.

-An Oxford punting pole from the Magdalen Bridge Boat House.
-The haunting geological formation of Heaven's Gate, on Tianmen Mountain, in
    Hunan Province, China.
-Salvador Dali's painting called *Triangular Time*, sort of.
-Angkor Wat, the great temples of Cambodia.
-Dante's Mt. Purgatory.
-A scored melody—other than "Las Vaquita Lullaby."
-Five M's hidden together in different ways throughout Mr. Mehan's Mildly Amusing
    Mythical Mammals.

## The Hardest Finds:
-Happy hunting, my sharp-eyed friends! Perhaps you can make your own lists to
    challenge other studious mammals! And don't forget: still more is hiding in the
    poems themselves!

# A *Giant* Natural History Mural

The Quecámbia painting holds a few creatures of old that we never knew, like those two wooly mammoths with mohawks and shades, which they put on after their awkwardest shaves. Scholars disagree whether the wooly mammoth's extinct due to climate change, men hunting their range, or disease—or as some think, some que-combination of these.

Key:

1. That huge, tongue-twisting, prehistoric beast—the largest land mammal of all time!—is called either the Indricotherium, the Paraceratherium, or, more simply, the Baluchitherium—phew! This hornless rhino's shoulder is as tall as the tallest man in history . . . times two!
2. A pair of Not-So-Wooly Mammoths with matching mohawks.
3. The four barbers are Diprotodons (Greek for "two front teeth"). These amiable, buck-toothed, and close-shaven mammals are the largest marsupials ever to have lived!
4. A Saber-Toothed Tiger reading the Prehistoric Times or the Washington Toast.
5. The Glyptodon is getting his shell removed by a Diprotodon. Glyptodons are like armadillos, but each the size of a compact car!
6. The Brontornis is the largest predatory bird ever. This nine-foot giant "Terror Bird" sat atop the food chain in Patagonia, a land named for a mythical race of giant humans, the Patagón. I doubt very much whether the snakes in the painting have one of *her* eggs.
7. The Quecámbia you already know! Too bad he wouldn't let his woolly quills go!

To join the mythical mammal community,
please visit our website
**www.mythicalmammals.com.**
Come find more hidden treasure
featuring your favorite mammals!